The
PARANOIAN

RAY SPROULE

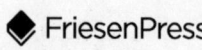 FriesenPress

One Printers Way
Altona, MB R0G 0B0
Canada

www.friesenpress.com

ISBN
978-1-03-915804-7 (Hardcover)
978-1-03-915803-0 (Paperback)
978-1-03-915805-4 (eBook)

1. FICTION, SCIENCE FICTION, ALIEN CONTACT

Distributed to the trade by The Ingram Book Company

Chapter 1 – The First Encounter

IT ALL BEGAN ON THE evening of a foggy autumn day in Linksville that dreary blue-collar suburb of Vancouver. I was a divorced counterfeit novelist freelancing for survival. "He's never writ anythin' worth a horse's puh-toot," I heard my landlord soullessly proclaim one day to the mailman stuffing mailboxes in the lobby. It made me want to stuff his mailbox, but I grudgingly had to admit, it loitered on the truth.

I was alone in the apartment feeling somewhat miserable, having just emerged from one of the mysterious blackouts that had been assailing me of late when there was a faint rap on the door, an intrusion I was strongly disposed to ignore. It had to be either the urchin from down the hall on a mission in quest of *oig kertins* — I never confessed to having any — or a salesperson for Muffin's *Old World Encyclopaedia of Practical Receipts, Processes, and Praxis*. The Muffin mercenaries had begun assaulting our modest apartment block, for some unfathomable reason, a few weeks back — with a truly Romanesque siege mentality.

I opened the door.

To my astonishment it was neither the small boy from down the hall nor a hooded Muffin emissary but a thin, delicate man in a thin, delicate suit. A pink suit, at least it resembled a suit, being remarkably well tailored to the subtlest contour of the man's slender frame. And, under this, this suit, at the essential surface of the man himself, was a skin — pale, limpid, and blue.

I blinked for several seconds utterly mesmerized.

It must have been longer for the man, ruffling his slipper-like shoes, spoke for the very first time.

"Might I come in?" he asked in a dainty, lilting voice.

"Why, why yes," I replied breathlessly.

With short smooth strides the little blue man glided past me and into the living room.

"Beautiful verdure," he murmured, referring to the profusion of potted plants so engulfing the room they distinctly conveyed the impression of feeding on the furniture.

"I don't overwater them," I replied humbly.

"*Très sage,*" he responded politely.

"My name is Lester Netherman," I said, boldly stepping forward.

There was always a tinge of regret when I presented someone my name, mainly because of the intolerable given name "Lester." My parents, both deceased now — not at my hand, I was cleared by the coroner's investigation — had decided that their first child

would not only be a girl but that she would be called "Esther,"
because of a long adoration of the actress Esther Williams, a senti-
ment shared by both of them. Needless to say, I was a disappoint-
ment to them and for some unfathomable reason, anointed me
"Lester" — and never had another child. This, however, was, in
a way, a veiled blessing. A sister named "Esther" would have been
doubly intolerable.

"And I am Pymm," he replied impassively. We shook hands.
His skin was soft to the touch and pulsated ever so gently. "I
am not from this world as you may have guessed," he added
with a chilling softness.

"I did not think so," I mumbled.

"Noo," he murmured, his lyrical voice a remarkable contrast to his stony expression. "I come from the planet Parr...
ahnn... ooha in the far-off galaxy of Urrt."

The planet's name was an almost unintelligible slur of "arrs"
and "ahs" and "oohas."

"Wh-what?" I stammered.

"Parr... ahnn... ooha," he repeated, his granite gray
eyes inspecting me clinically. "Ah well, the closest word in
earth-tongue is, I believe, either 'Piranha' or 'Paranoia'. You
choose, Lester."

My heart pounded wildly.

Had I heard him correctly?

"Make it Paranoia," I finally managed to mutter. "I hate fish."

Without asking, he seated himself in the wooden rocking
chair in the shadow of the monster philodendron with the
broad groping leaves.

I sat down on the sofa, got up, and sat down again, then got up again, and out of desperation, went into the kitchen and put on the kettle.

"Do you drink tea?" I grunted upon returning to the living room.

"*Mais oui,*" he purred.

The conversation continued fitfully. Pymm was overly cautious — with the disconcerting habit of interjecting the occasional French expression into his conversation — and I of course, was a light-year away from being a polished host.

Ever since my wife had left, taking our infant son with her — he had just begun to crawl, I, of course, had been crawling all my life — I found potted plants far more comfortable to be around than humans.

Eventually, Pymm, with lowered head, launched into a long narration, and my mind began to wander — though I did interject the occasional "oh?", "yes," and "hmm" — as well as an intermittent "*oui*" — into the conversation.

Finally, the phrase "First Crossing" jarred me to attention.

Was the little blue man referring to a spaceship? I wondered.

"Lester, it was *si tragique,*" he continued mournfully. "Did you hear about it in the news?"

"N-n-no," I stammered.

Not only was I unsure of what he was referring to, but I had little interest in current events. I had no use for television, though I did glance at the front page of the local newspaper from time to time and had seen absolutely nothing about crossings, or little blue men. Surely with any form of alien incursion onto Earth, newspapers would have machine-gunned out the headlines: "Extraterrestrial Landings! Little Blue Men from Outer Space!; No Need to Panic, but We're Being Invaded!" and so on, but no, I had seen no such things.

Then, after mulling the idea over in my mind, I did recall something my landlord had said, in the lobby, a few days back, something about alien beings landing in the United States. Only one of the creatures had supposedly survived the landing and was being held incommunicado — in a dungeon cell under Mount Rushmore. The story was reputedly being quashed by U.S. authorities to avoid widespread panic. My landlord had picked up the information on his Citizen's Band radio, and consequently, believed every fragment of the story, while I — being skeptical of both landlords and CB radios — had dismissed it utterly.

But now, with a shivering little blue man sitting in front of me, I felt a sudden panic.

"You, you," I sputtered, "you're the sole survivor?"

"Noo," said Pymm with a cold depths-of-outer-space stare. "Noo one survived from the *First Crossing*."

"But there was a rumor that…?"

"Ooh, Broom survived for a time, but he's dead now."

"I'm sorry."

"I knoow."

"You can read minds?" I asked, my pulse suddenly quickening — being amply conditioned to expect as much from any alien creature.

What other, private thoughts, could he detect? I wondered.

"Noo, you just look sad," he murmured.

Should I tell him I always looked sad? No, that, in itself, would have been sad.

The kettle in the kitchen began to whistle.

Pymm's tiny ears perked up.

"Don't be alarmed," I said soothingly, "it's just the water boiling for the tea." Chuckling nervously, I entered the kitchen, returning a moment later with the tea service tray, and poured the mint tea into my precious made-in-Bulgaria teacups — before asking the obvious question. "If no one survived, how did you get here, Pymm?"

Pymm's opaque blue skin deepened.

"Ooh! I am from the *Second Crossing.*"

"The Second Coming?"

"Noo, the *Second Crossing.* It's our spaceship, Lester. Broom signaled home from *his* spaceship, the *First Crossing,* just before his death. We left immediately to investigate and continue their mission."

"We," I cried. "You mean there are more of you?"

Scores of little blue men suddenly materialized before my eyes, scurrying about the surface of the Earth, rapping on doors in a massive ground-roots invasion — and I had thought the Muffin Mercenaries a threat to the planet!

"Just my *suum-mate,* Poothy."

"And where is he?" I asked, dreading another rap on the door.

"She!" snapped Pymm. "Poothy remained in *la soucoupe.*"

"The what?"

"The flying saucer. Should I have said *le saucer?*"

"I don't know," I confessed. "My own French is *terrible*."

"*Ooh la la!*"

I relaxed. It wasn't quite the invasion I had visualized.

"Tell me, Pymm, why do you insert these French phrases into your speech from time to time? Frankly, it's a little disconcerting."

"Ooh," moaned Pymm. "But there are soo many languages on Earth, it's very confusing. There is only one language on Paranoia."

"Still, you do seem to communicate very well."

"*Da!*" replied Pymm, before quickly adding, "Oops, sorry, Lester, I'll try to concentrate better. And yith, we Paranoians doo have a special facility for speech. We're not so good with physical endeavors, however, especially in the area of what you call *sports*. Your focus on hitting balls, balls of all kinds is, well, very weird.

"Now that you mention it," I conceded, "we do seem to have an odd obsession with balls."

"Yith, and there's that sport where you hit balls with feathers."

"We hit balls with feathers?" I mumbled, puzzled. "Oh, you're referring to badminton. We call them *birdies*."

"Disgusting!" hissed Pymm.

"Tell me more about the *First Crossing*," I said, desperately wanting to leave the subject of balls — especially balls with feathers.

"*Eh bien!* The *First Crossing* landed in a place you call Nevada."

"Ah yes, I've been to Reno once — on a bus tour."

"Vast stretches of sand, *très formidable*!"

"Is there any sand on Paranoia?" I asked, desperately searching for an appropriate question to ask.

"Very little."

"Did it take long for you to reach Earth?"

"Noo, not for *un saucer* powered by an *orgasm*," purred Pymm.

"Orgasm?" I croaked, choking on my tea.

"Yith. Paranoian *orgasms* are powerful propellants."

"Remarkable! You know, that on Earth an orgasm is …?"

"I knoow," murmured Pymm, who was rocking gently back and forth now. "Broom signaled that while he was exploring the desert on foot — Elsymm, his *suum-mate,* having remained in *le saucer* — an ancient aircraft flew directly overhead."

"A biplane?" I blurted out.

"*Non!* It was a modern warplane but armed with ancient weapons."

"Oh," I replied — *wondering if those "ancient weapons" could have been "Greek balls of fire."*

"Yith, Lester, and when the warplane had gone, Broom continued exploring in the vicinity of *le saucer.*"

"Pymm, a minor point perhaps, given the historic nature of your visit to Earth, but I do detest the name Lester."

"You detest your name?"

"Yith, I mean yes."

"Would you like me to shorten it to Esther?"

"That's even worse, Pymm, and it's hardly shorter. Just call me Netherman, everyone here on Earth does."

"You know everyone on Earth?"

"No, Pymm. It's just an expression."

"Oh! Now, if I may return to my story? While Broom was exploring the area — carrying a *looking-stick* with sensors analyzing features both above and below the ground — more warplanes appeared, swarming across the sky, like *burgees*."

"*Burgees?*"

"Yith, huge raucous Paranoian birds, and though ferocious-looking, they are nevertheless quite harmless — unless they accidentally sit on you."

"There are no such birds on Earth, as far as I know, but I know a few people like that," I replied.

"They sit on you?"

"Sometimes."

There was a bully in my high school who liked to sit on kids. He never sat on me, though — not that I could recall. It seemed to be my only memory of high school, or before that, for that matter.

"Well," continued Pymm, "the warplanes were dipping in and out, zooming down close to the ground, threateningly — though *le saucer* itself was safe enough, being protected by its alien-shield."

"Heavens! An alien-shield?"

"Yith, Netherman. It's a protective shield that not only averts physical attacks, but that sends thought impulses through space. I was going to say thought waves, but waves require a medium, and these impulses do not require a medium, except space, if you wish to consider it a medium, which it is, of sorts."

"You're getting rather technical, Pymm," I admonished.

"Sorry, Esther. Oops, I mean, Netherman."

"What are these thought impulses like?"

"It's complicated, but in short, they make earthlings sick. In any case, the warplanes suddenly began firing projectiles at the *First Crossing*. Broom barely managed to reenter *le saucer* before moving to another location."

"The warplanes didn't chase after it?"

"Noo, they couldn't. As soon as Broom touched *le saucer's* controls, it shifted instantaneously to a different set of coordinates."

"Wow! So Broom escaped. How do you know all this?"

"Broom sent regular signals back to Paranoia."

"But wait, didn't you say that they had died?"

"They did, later, after returning to the original landing site."

"Goodness, they returned?"

"Yith, two days later, at night, thinking it would be safer."

"And there were no warplanes patrolling the site?"

"Noo, not at first."

"But why did they go back, Pymm?"

"They returned to investigate something highly unusual, something they had seen during their first landing, some kind of strange sand creature."

"Oh my God! Was it a Gila monster?"

"We never found out, Netherman. There was no further communication between us for another eight hours, and then Broom sent his final set of transmissions, intermittent and highly garbled. There were two intelligible fragments 'returned to' and 'warplanes again,' followed by a short silence, and then more fragments stating that they had been attacked, Elsymm had perished, and that he himself was mortally wounded. The final message was that he had managed to reenter the *First Crossing* and bury it deep in the sand."

"He could do that?"

"Yith, the *First Crossing's orgasm* was still fully functional."

"And yet the transmissions were garbled?"

"Something else might have disturbed them," replied Pymm. "In any case, when Poothy and I reached Earth, we landed exactly where the *First Crossing* had landed, but found nothing but barren desert — and soo much sand. Our scanner detected the buried *First Crossing* with one dead body on board, that of Broom according to his genetic makeup."

"And Elsymm's body?"

"Broom had been forced to leave her body behind on the sand outside the *First Crossing*, but when we arrived, we couldn't find it."

"It wasn't hidden just under the sand? The wind does drift the sand about," I offered.

I had considered suggesting that maybe some animal had ravaged the body, and scattered the remains about, but decided against it.

"*Non! Pas du tout!* We scanned the entire area."

It then occurred to me that some U.S. government agency might have found and removed the body. Maybe the rumour on my landlord's CB wasn't so nonsensical after all. I didn't have the heart to tell Pymm of my suspicions, any of them.

"Did you try to reach Broom, to dig out the spaceship?"

"Noo! He was dead, and it was safer to keep the *First Crossing* buried to avoid attracting further attention."

"You mean from the authorities?"

"*Oui, mon vieux.* After all, they did kill poor Broom and Elsymm."

"One thing that puzzles me, Pymm," I said, "was why there was no U.S. government presence on the scene, either air force or army, when you and the *Second Crossing* arrived? That seems strange to me."

"Please, noo more talk," he moaned. "The subject is *tellement dérangeant, tellement dérangeant.*"

Pymm was rocking gently back and forth now — the philodendron having gradually cantilevered out over him, as though striving for a more advantageous eavesdropping position.

Both the rocking and the philodendron's creepy creeping forward had a hypnotic effect on me, and soon, my vision became increasingly blurry, until finally — I lost all consciousness.

Chapter 2 – Paranoia

WHERE AM I? I THOUGHT.

It was cool.

I seemed to be lying down, but not upon a bed or lounging chair, but suspended in air in some fashion or other. There was no pressure against my body, just suspension.

I easily shifted position.

How could this be? I wondered.

Then Pymm walked into the, the what? It wasn't a normal room, though it seemed like one, without walls and a ceiling, and even a floor — nothingness in every direction.

"Hello, Noothy, soo glad you're awake," murmured Pymm.

"Noothy?" I blustered, "but my name is Netherman?"

Pymm hesitated.

"Ah yith, sorry."

"And where is this, this place?"

"You are in Ataraxia. It's a hospital of sorts, a place of recovery."

"A hospital?" I gasped. "My God! What planet are we on?"

"You're on Paranoia, of course," murmured Pymm, mystified. "Look around you. Where else could you be?"

And, indeed, Pymm seemed to be right for there was nothing Earth-like about my surroundings.

"But, Pymm, this can't be happening. We were just having a pleasant conversation in my apartment in Linksville. You just dropped in — uninvited, I might say."

"And where is this Linksville?"

"Why, it's on planet Earth, of course."

"As far as I know, Noothy, sorry, I mean Netherman, there is no planet Earth. I think that somehow you are confusing it with Urrt, the galaxy we're in."

"Damn you, Pymm, you Shanghaied me!" I cried desperately.

"What is this 'Shanghai' thing?"

"It means that you kidnapped me, Pymm."

"I-I don't think so," murmured Pymm, apparently confused.

"And what is this recovery you talk of — recovery from what?"

"Ooh. Noothy, you are still very ..."

"Stop calling me that!" I shouted. "My name is Netherman."

"Okay then, Netherman," replied Pymm contritely. "But you are still very ill and recovery will take time. You need to sleep, restore your health. I'll return later to see how you're doing."

"Don't leave me, Pymm!" I cried. "Please don't leave."

But Pymm had quickly dissolved into the nothingness.

Struggling to my feet, I took a few tentative steps forward, mysteriously supported, though there seemed to be nothing underfoot. A few more steps led into a long, narrow hallway, with walls, thank God, and a floor, everything seemingly normal now — yet with a pervading strangeness to it all.

I came to a window, and peering through it, looked out upon what seemed to be a garden — with a multitude of distorted oddly shaped trees, bushes, and flowering plants, all under a bright sun and an unnaturally tinted deep-sea green sky.

What had Pymm said, that I was ill, and needed to recover? Recover? From what? And where was I? Was I truly on Paranoia? The world I now looked out upon, seemingly so real, was certainly not Earth.

My last clear memory, apart from Pymm's visiting me on Earth, was of the boy from down the hallway on his quest for oig *kertins. I couldn't remember much else about Earth, and that terrified me. And how had I ended up here on this strange planet, if indeed I was on some strange planet? Had Pymm somehow, either drugged or mesmerized me and brought me here aboard his spaceship — his saucer?*

Suddenly from down the hallway, I saw someone approaching, someone bent over, seemingly an invalid, in a puffy green dressing gown that covered most of him, or her, or it. As the specter neared, it raised its head and a round face smiled at me — *a round blue Paranoian face!*

The creature continued on past as though I was no stranger to it, and moreover, belonged in that hallway. And then for the first time I noticed that I, too, wore a puffy green dressing gown.

I scurried back to the relative comfort of my "room," and once there, began wondering where I had lain down, seeing only nothingness. Then slowly, a shadowy gray form appeared, eventually materializing into a kind of reclining couch.

I touched it. It was solid enough. I wearily lay down. It supported me. I rested.

Moments later as I lay staring fixedly in one direction, a wall seemed to materialize. I rose and stroked it, and it, too, was solid enough, but yielding, also, as though, with a little effort on my part, I could make it disappear.

Then I gradually became aware that my mind was forming these objects around me, first the couch, then the wall, and when they finally appeared, they were substantial enough.

The realization was powerfully thrilling — and terrifying!

As though borne by some unconscious thought, a mirror suddenly appeared before me, suspended in air, and in it, a reflection — a reflection of a thin blue man!

I heard someone scream then realized — *that I was the one who had screamed!* My body turned to rubber.

I blacked out.

Chapter 3 – The First Encounter Resumed

WHEN I REGAINED CONSCIOUSNESS, I was back in my living room in Linksville. Pymm was sitting in the rocking chair under the umbrella of the philodendron, staring at me with a concerned look.

"Damn it, Pymm," I cried. "What just happened?"

"I'm not sure, Netherman," he murmured. "For a moment, you were sitting upright, totally unresponsive, no body movement, no quivering of the eyes."

"For how long was this?"

"A few minutes only, but you seemed to have recovered now."

I took a deep breath, immensely relieved at being back on Earth again, and especially, not being Shanghaied. But I certainly wasn't going to tell Pymm what I had dreamt, or imagined.

Nightmares were too personal to share with an alien visitor — even though they were part of that nightmare.

"Do you often have these, these odd moments?" asked Pymm.

"No, nothing like this has happened before, though frankly, Pymm, my memory seems to be fading. I only remember a few things, recent things, but almost nothing of my past."

I carefully inspected the creature that had so mystically materialized on my doorstep.

Was he what he said he was, a friendly being from the planet Paranoia, or was he an impostor, a clever makeup artist perpetrating some elaborate and weird hoax?

But no, that was not the case. I could sense with every fiber of my being, every fat cell, every nerve ending in my body, that the creature so primly propped up in the rocking chair before me was, indeed, what he said he was — a being from another world.

But, I was suspicious of his motives.

Was the story he told about the First Crossing *true? I wondered. And what of the* Second Crossing, *what was its true purpose for visiting Earth? And even more frightening was why he had chosen my particular door to knock upon. No creature in the universe could be as innocent as Pymm appeared.*

A direct approach seemed best.

"So tell me, Pymm, why did you come to Earth in the first place?"

"We Paranoians are curious creatures," he replied, casually stroking an arm of the rocking chair with his spindle fingertips.

"You certainly are aggressive enough," I said icily.

"We're not aggressive, Netherman, we're merely inquisitive," replied Pymm defensively. "We have an insatiable thirst for truth much as you earthlings thirst for money and happiness. It is a basic Paranoian tenet that truth is more fundamental than well-being. We send hundreds of crossings into the universe, to countless planets, in this pursuit of truth."

"How did you ever find out about Earth, that we even existed?"

"Why, Netherman, it was you who signaled us."

"No? Whatever do you mean?" I barked.

What was the insipid little man talking about?

"Don't you know that your electronic devices, radios and televisions, and such things, have been radiating signals into the universe for decades now, in an immense ever-expanding sphere?" he murmured. "The first signals we received were highly garbled, almost indecipherable, but they did reveal the presence of more or less intelligent beings on your planet. In time, as our scanners improved, the signals became clearer." Pymm stopped rocking suddenly. "Do you remember a cinema called *Duck Soup?*" he quipped.

"*Duck Soup!*" I cried. "You mean that old Marx brothers movie?"

"Why yith, Netherman, it gave us our very first glimpse into the nature of you earthlings?"

"That is astounding!"

"Oh yith, the Marx brothers caused quite a stir on Paranoia," murmured Pymm, his lithesome frame quivering with emotion. "For a time we thought all earthlings were silly, bizarre creatures. Later, we discovered that, in fact, most earth-lings were silly and bizarre, but in an entirely different way."

Refilling Pymm's teacup, I wondered what other intriguing revelations the rascal had in store for me. I totally agreed with his "silly and bizarre" comment, however.

"Do you have television on your planet?" I eventually asked.

"Noo," responded Pymm, with crystalline coolness. "We did eons ago but then discovered that these television devices cause irreversible wrinkle-convolutions in the brain."

"Gore Vidal does refer to television as 'moving wallpaper.'"

"Who is this Gore Vidal?"

"He's a famous earthling novelist."

"*Comme toi*, Netherman?"

"Not exactly, Pymm," I said, with a light laugh.

"But Netherman," whispered Pymm in his devilishly seduc-tive voice, "we've heard of you on Paranoia."

Thin icicle chills knifed through me.

What in heavens did the wicked little blue man mean? I did not want to be "heard of" on Paranoia, or any other alien planet for that matter, though I could have accepted a little more "heard of" here on Earth.

"That is why I visited you, specifically, *mon vieux*," con-tinued Pymm, "to meet Lester Netherman, author of *The Earth Eaters.*"

Stunned by the revelation, coming so unexpectedly, I stared vulnerably at Pymm while painful memories stirred in my brain.

"*The Earth Eaters?*" I eventually mumbled.

The Earth Eaters *was my very first attempt at a novel — more of a long short story, really, a science-fiction tale about a colony of giant mutant bacteria thriving below the Earth's crust, eating away at the rock and soil, gradually undermining the Earth's superstructure, all according to intelligent design. Their ultimate plan was to take over the world by threatening mankind with extinction, in particular, mankind's space-science technology, and then fly off into space where the moon and the other planets waited to be feasted upon.*

Unfortunately, the novel had been published by an obscure publishing house called Oolie Oolie Books, unfortunate because — the miniature publishing house printed just enough copies to garner the novel sufficient ridicule that no one took me seriously ever after.

And now, my bastard novel was coming back to haunt me!

"My memory's a bit fuzzy," I breathed.

"It's those wrinkle-convolutions," murmured Pymm. "You were courageous, though, warning earth of the danger."

"Danger?" I snorted. "What on Earth do you mean?"

Pymm laughed in his soft fluting mildly irritating manner.

"Ooh! You did not mean earth-eating creatures literally, Netherman. Your warning was far subtler."

"Frankly, Pymm, I don't know what you're talking about," I muttered, completely mystified. "It was just a dumb novel."

There was no chance to pursue the matter, however, for without warning, Pymm sprang from the rocking chair.

"I must leave," he murmured, a sense of urgency in his voice.

"But you can't," I protested, involuntarily gripping his shoulder. "You haven't finished explaining…"

"My deepest regrets, Netherman, but I must leave."

"But where will you go?"

"Poothy and I shall be visiting the Dark Continent next."

"Do you mean Africa?" I asked, somewhat bewildered.

"Yith, according to our research, it's the Earth's last remaining unexplored continent."

"But Africa's not unexplored, Pymm," I protested. "Your information is way out-of-date, and I still have so many questions."

"We will return, I promise, after scanning Africa," he murmured.

And then, in spite of my continued protests, Pymm strutted nimbly towards the door and left — without a single *au revoir*.

With a tall glass of mint tea and a jelly donut for nourishment, I spent the next hour lost in philosophic immobility, dozing in and out of reality, slowly recuperating from the shock of my first encounter with the Man from Paranoia.

Chapter 4 – The Second Encounter

TWO DAYS LATER I WAS awakened from a deep and troublesome sleep — wherein I dreamt of disparate worlds and peculiar realities — by a frantic rapping on my apartment door.

It was Pymm with his pink outfit disheveled, and — in sharp contrast to his overall pink-on-blue-ness — he brandished a brand-new black Fedora, giving him a distinctly Earthy and rakish George Raft air.

He made a beeline for the rocking chair where the suddenly revitalized monster philodendron with the broad groping leaves, eased protectively out towards him.

"Did you tussle with a lion?" I asked, amused, and relieved, by his sudden re-appearance, admittedly having missed him.

"*Malheureusement, non,*" he moped. "I believed that Africa was totally covered in jungles, but all we saw was sand, vast stretches of it. What a depressing planet!"

"You must have visited the Sahara," I said, suppressing a laugh.

"There is something else that disturbs me," he continued, eyeing me with glacial coldness. "It's just that during my numerous sorties over your planet, we have been sighted hundreds of times by earthlings, and still, there is noo mention of us in Earth's news media."

"You want more attention?"

"Noo, not particularly, but it does hurt one's feelings."

"We all want to be noticed, I suppose."

"Just a little attention would be nice."

"Even after the attack on the *First Crossing*?"

"After some thought, Netherman, I now believe that the attack on the *First Crossing* was a mistake, a misunderstanding by your Earth authorities, and if they had known that we Paranoians had come in peace, our reception would have been different."

"Maybe so," I said, skeptically, "but remember, we earthlings are, in your own words, 'silly and bizarre.'"

"I truly don't understand earthlings," moaned Pymm.

"I don't understand us either, Pymm," I confessed. "We defy interpretation, especially if it's rational interpretation. It seems that there's a kind of belief-barrier to break through. An earthling won't believe anything unless everyone else believes it, too, regardless of how logical it is or how much sense it makes."

In spite of my cynicism, mild though it was, I was sympathetic to Pymm's predicament, and also had wondered at how little attention the little blue man's visit to Earth had fostered. And then I had a moment of inspiration.

Maybe what Pymm needed was more exposure!

"What do you say to a radio interview?" I blurted out. "I believe I can arrange for you to appear on a local radio talk show."

"A talk show, what's that?" quivered Pymm.

"There are no talk shows on Paranoia? Oh my, that is backward!" I chided, going on to explain the wonders of a radio audience telephoning in questions to a host, often someone of some stature — though that would not be the case, if the person I had in mind were available.

"Would that help in introducing our presence here on Earth?"

"It's a start, Pymm," I replied.

"But I thought I had already started?"

"Yes, Pymm, but there's something invisible about you, something I can't quite figure out."

"But, Netherman, why not arrange something on television?" the ungracious little man countered.

In a dark corner of the living room there lurked a mature Venus fly-trap plant, dug out of a remote North Carolinian bog — while I was on vacation some years back, or so I seem to recall, though my recollection was fuzzy. Its leaf-blade resembled a steel trap in its action, the marginal bristles interlocking like teeth. Three pairs of trigger-hairs lined the upper leaf surface, and when one of them was touched, ever so lightly, the trap slammed shut, viscous fluids poured forth, and the unfortunate prey was digested. I only refer to this, this incidental member of my floral community, because, at that particular moment in time, I had the overwhelming urge to lift my extraterrestrial guest up bodily — and screw him headlong into the beckoning mouth of the carnivorous plant.

Television was a step too far for someone of my limited influence.

Our only reasonable shot for exposure of any kind was an interview with local CKLV radio host Rufus Mulligan. Rufus was a perennially lost soul with a taste for the bizarre. It was worth a try. A quick call to the radio station led immediately — as though by divine, or perhaps, extraterrestrial, intervention — to the great man, himself.

"A creature from outer space, you say? Hmm! We do have quite a schedule already planned, you understand."

After a very short period of pleading on my part, we made the necessary arrangements.

In afterthought, I realized that Mr. Mulligan had required little persuasion, and wondered as to how extensive his "quite a schedule already planned" really was.

Later that evening, long after Pymm had departed, I spent an hour sipping mint tea and ruminating over earlier events. Pymm had given only a lukewarm promise to appear at the CKLV studio at the appointed hour.

Would he show up? I wondered.

I had asked him if he would have trouble finding the studio. His reply had been: "We found Earth, didn't we?"

And Rufus Mulligan was a puzzle also.

He had shown little interest in Pymm, either as a person, or even a phenomenon. There were no "Where is he from?" or "What does he look like?" questions, indicating genuine interest in having an extraterrestrial guest on his show. And when I began volunteering information regarding Pymm, he had rudely interrupted me with a curt "Can he speak English?"

"He can speak all languages," I had replied, angry at his curtness.

"All of them?"

"Yes, without exception."

"Look, Needleman..."

"It's Netherman!" I had snapped back.

"Yeah, well, English is all he needs, and it doesn't have to be that great either," he had replied, wheezing audibly before hanging up.

"Drink that!" I muttered grumpily to myself, tossing the remainder of my mint tea into the philodendron pot.

Plants were better companions than pets, especially dogs. For one thing, they didn't bark as much — even when you doused them with tea.

Chapter 5 – The Talk Show

RUFUS MULLIGAN WAS A TORMENTED man cursed with a singular affliction — he gained weight inexorably and for no apparent reason. It had all started two years ago when the fibula bone in his left leg, just below the knee, had been crushed in a hydraulic wine-press — how it got there was never revealed — and an artificial segment had been inserted. From that fateful moment on, his bulk had grown inexorably. A year later, with the scales pressing three-hundred pounds, he had gone on an eight-hundred calorie per day starvation diet, no salt, sugar, or bread, but still his form continued to burgeon outward. And no doctor, mystic, or naturalist, out of scores consulted, had the faintest inkling of a cure or explanation for the bizarre disorder.

Today, at a portentous four-hundred-and-fifty pounds, Rufus Mulligan stubbornly refused to discuss his unique predicament with anyone, doctor or friend alike — stoically determined to accept whatever fate had in store for him.

It wasn't quite the Death of Ivan Ilyich scenario, but it was close.

In order to accommodate the great man while hosting his talk show, a specially reinforced circular stool with five stout cast-iron legs had been constructed, and upon this roost, the talk-show king prevailed.

I watched the proceedings from the anonymity of a stool in a dark corner of the studio, not wanting to interfere in any way, though aware, that we all influence our surroundings in some small way or other. I was a staunch believer in Heisenberg's Uncertainty Principle and was quite taken by its overall applicability, even in the present circumstances.

I often experienced these moments of philosophic introspection.

"A virtuous greeting to y'all, hee, hee," began Rufus Mulligan. "It's time for torrid talk, and casual conversation, too, here on Mully's Way! Hi! I'm your host, Rufus Mulligan, on CKLV, coming to you live from the panoramic flats of Linksville, B.C. — Chain-Link Capital of the Universe. To-night for your listening pleasure, and diversion, we've a guest who's, well simply put — extraterrestrial. Yes, my wee friends, this fine starlit night, Old Rufus promises you a tantalizing frenzy of an evening with a real hissing spitting man from outer space! Yes indeed, a veritable Martian, by the name of Mr. Pymm. No, no, don't touch that dial. Portly Rufus's not spaced out, or... oh wait, a cat in a tweed suit's pointing a bony paw at me. What? There's a correction on the Martian bit? Para... Paranoia? You're kidding? Hey! Sorry, folks. Apparently, our visitor is not from Mars, but rather from some offbeat planet called Paranoia. Can you believe it? In any case, as an appetizer, we've the privilege of having Professor Peyronie from the University of Bologna with us in the studio tonight to prepare us for the big event. Welcome, *professore*."

"Delighted, *Signor Rufus*," replied the academic, his neck swiveling like an ostrich's — a miniature ostrich. The professor was a small man but agile.

"Tell us, *professore*, what is your area of expertise?"

"I am *un esperto* in the arena of *astronomia*," replied the Italian, his eyes gleaming like stars of the first magnitude.

"Perhaps you could begin, *professore*, by telling us where this, this planet Paranoia is located in this vast universe of ours?"

"Ah, *sì, signore*, apparently thees planet Paranoia, she lie in *una gallassia, molto passato*. She has never been espied *otticamente*."

"You mean by telescope?"

"*Sì, telescopio*. Paranoia, she ees *molto, molto lontano*."

"So, if it's so far away, how do we know this planet even exists?"

"*Buona questione!*" replied the professor with gusto. "*Due astronomi — professsori Faustdick e Luft —* they have inferred eets *esistenza* by *un vasto compendio…*"

"A what?" interjected Mulligan.

"*Lotsa dati, signore*."

"Ahh!"

"*Per favore, il pianeto*, Paranoia, ees een *la gallassia* Biagio A."

"Never heard of it," grunted Mulligan.

"Eet ees the 'stuttering' *gallassia, signore*."

"Stuttering?"

"*Sì, signore.* Eet stutters — to thee eye, not thee ear."

"Frankly, *professore,* that sounds nuts," said Mulligan.

"It's called Urrt," whispered Pymm plaintively. "Paranoia is in the galaxy of Urrt."

But no one seemed to have heard him.

"It's time for a word from Adolf Mueller's Chain-Link Fences," announced Rufus Mulligan suddenly, his terraced jowls tightening visibly, indicating the strain he was under. "If you've got a hankerin' for chain, then Adolf Mueller's the name."

Off the air, tiny beads of sweat cascaded down Mulligan's cheeks.

Fractured fingernails beat a nervous tattoo on the tabletop.

"Care for an espresso?" he asked, turning to Pymm.

"Noo," bleated the Paranoian, evidently also ill-at-ease.

"Don't be so glum, Pymm. Your turn's coming up."

I felt sorry for Pymm. He was far more nervous than appeared on the surface. But the interview did not necessarily have to be a disaster, not if, not if? The question hung in the air. I really wasn't sure what could keep it from being a disaster.

Then suddenly, I began to wonder. How did the Italian professor, as well as the astronomical world at large, know about the planet Paranoia's existence, and even the galaxy it was in?

Was all this really happening?

And then I must have dozed off, for sometime later I awoke coiled up on the floor. No one seemed to have noticed, so I slid back onto my stool. The talk show was now in full swing, but disappointingly enough, Rufus Mulligan's one-on-one interview with Pymm had ended.

"Well, folks, that was indeed a nice interview with Mr. Pymm," boomed Mulligan, "but now, the moment we have all been waiting for has finally arrived. My pulse quickens in anticipation, for — it's time to open up our boards to you common folks out there — and add your voices to the grand cosmic symphony of *upness*, *downess*, *strangeness*, and *charm* that is at the very core of our universe. Let us begin!"

"And I am ready, *signore*," chimed Profesor Peyronie eagerly.

"Not you, *professore*, the Paranoian," retorted Mulligan.

"Ah *sì*," replied a disappointed *Italiano*.

"And yes, folks, we are waiting breathlessly for that first earthling in our audience to be the one to converse directly with Mr. Pymm — the Man from Paranoia?"

A long silence ensued.

"Speak up, man, give us your name," barked Mulligan.

"Wittol Tucker from over Langley way?" drawled a voice finally.

"Your question, sir?" rumbled Mulligan.

"'Ow'd 'e git 'ere?" came the hesitant reply.

"*Un saucer*," hissed Pymm, absentmindedly lapsing into French.

"Whaa?"bleated the man.

"*Un ovoidale* spacesheep, *signore*," interjected the professor.

"Ovoi…?" mumbled Mr. Tucker.

"It's a flying saucer, Mr. Farmer," interjected Mulligan.

"The name's Tucker, sir," grumbled the voice. "Now kin yah tell me what kind a motor 'as it got?"

"*Le saucer* is powered by an *orgasm*," replied Pymm smoothly, tilting his black Fedora forward over his eyes.

"Well now," said Rufus Mulligan, laughing gleefully. "Did you hear what the creature said?"

"Never 'eard a one," droned Wittol Tucker. "Now then, is thet flyin' saucer a yers parked over in a field in Cloverdale?"

"*Le saucer* rests in a grassy meadow in…" Pymm began to say.

"Not on the air!" screamed Mulligan, leaning towards Pymm and whispering, "You don't want earthlings swarming all over your spaceship, do you?"

"Noo," murmured Pymm.

"Okay then, wise up," snapped Mulligan.

"Sorry, Rufus," said Pymm tamely.

"Next caller!" bellowed Mulligan, wiping his brow with a dank shirtsleeve.

"Am I getting through, can you hear me?" quivered a male voice, through mild static. "I'm calling from way over in Yelm."

"And where's that, my good man?" asked Mulligan apprehensively.

"It's kind of you to inquire, sir. We've a nice little commune here — a piece of heaven, as one might say — over near the Yelm River?"

"Ah yes, you're in Yelm County, state of Washington, of course," replied Mulligan solicitously. "What can we do for you neighbor?"

"Well, we just heard about this, this marvelous creature from outer space, and of course we just had to call."

"Your question?" asked Mulligan acidly.

"Ah yes, I'm sure that all of us here on Earth would like to know what the creature looks like?"

Rufus Mulligan gave Pymm a skittish glance.

"Since you ask," replied Rufus Mulligan warily, "Mr. Pymm is a thin package about sixteen hands high, with distinctly blue skin."

"Is he horsey-like? You did say 'hands'?"

"Yeah, I did. Sorry. No, he's not horsey-like in any way."

"And you said his skin is blue?"

"I did, sir."

"What kind of blue?"

"Oh, I don't know," muttered Mulligan, growing impatient.

"Heavens!" chided the voice. "There are so many shades of blue. There's azure blue, damson blue, and even eggshell blue. Good God! It could be robin's-egg blue, for all we know."

"Next!" boomed Mulligan.

"Dr. Mort speaking," asserted a cutting male voice, "chief pathologist at Linksville General."

"And what can we do for *you*?" asked Mulligan breezily.

"Frankly speaking, I'd like to dissect your guest."

A shocked silence followed, during which time, the fatty creases in Rufus Mulligan's face combined to form a sketch of porcine horror.

"You can't do that, doc," replied Mulligan coolly.

"Why not? I'm a certified pathologist."

"Well, it does seem a bit premature."

"Perhaps, you're right. Call if the situation changes."

The line went dead.

"One never knows," sighed Mulligan, gawking aimlessly about the room. "Bring on the next bozo."

"Wilbur Bunch at your service, sir," announced a strident voice. "President of the S.L.U."

"What in God's Gehenna is the S.L.U.?" groaned Mulligan.

"Never heard of us, eh? We're the Shaarrimpmen's Labor Union," snapped Wilbur Bunch, with shark-like savagery. "We work the shaarrimp boats offa the coast, eh? I'm calling 'bout them allegations made against my person, anonymously, in the *Chronicle*, a couple a days past, and I wanna say right here and now — I fully intend to find out who the alligator is!"

Rufus Mulligan signaled for the taped commercial.

"What the fuck's going on?" he snarled. "Don't they realize who our guest is?"

"*Calmati, calmati*," cautioned Professor Peyronie soothingly. "You ees *meraviglioso*."

"Yeah, maybe," fretted Mulligan, casting a wary glance in Pymm's direction — but the little blue man was gazing absentmindedly off into space. How far, no one really knew. "Hopefully our next caller has something meaningful to offer. The lines are open, speak up, please," continued Rufus Mulligan.

"Hu-hullo?" said a childlike voice, evidently, that of a little girl.

"Speak up, you're on the air."

"Hullo?"

"Tell us your name, please."

An inordinately long pause followed.

"My name's Annabelle," quivered the voice, finally.

Rufus Mulligan was reaching to terminate the call, when a frantic signal from the producer stopped him. It was not politic to cut off children prematurely — especially little girls with quivering voices.

"Annabelle what?" growled Rufus Mulligan.

"I-I don't reemumba."

"Where's your mommy, Annabelle?"

"My mommy's dead."

"Dead, as in she's never coming back?"

"Yeth."

"But why did you call us, Annabelle?"

"I'm hungry," replied Annabelle with a sniffle.

"Shit!" moaned Mulligan, ending the call.

Neither patience nor social concern was a virtue in Rufus Mulligan's scheme of things, even when little boys and girls were involved. "We are all God's creatures," he had once said, "therein lies our problem." And on another occasion, "Little boys and little girls are nothing but tiny adults." It was a fine point! And the more I got to know Rufus Mulligan, the more I grew to understand him, and even like him — and even agree on his position regarding little boys and girls.

The talk show had progressed in its undulating, unpredictable, and utterly deflating fashion, and Rufus Mulligan's doughy bulk had pancaked out on his specially reinforced stool — while I had been dozing in and out, often wondering where I actually was — when suddenly I heard Rufus Mulligan scream.

"For Christ's sake, Ezekial, why is every damn thing about religion with you?"

"My question is for the alien visitor, not you, Mr. Mulligan," replied the caller calmly. "Tell me, is it possible that you were sent here to Earth by our almighty God?"

"I really don't think so," replied Pymm cautiously.

"Why? Don't you believe in God, or some form of divine being?"

"Noo, not personally, though some Paranoians believe in *Goor*."

"Good God, what's that?"

"*Goor* is a kind of universal mystical grandparent."

"All powerful and divine?"

"Far from it," murmured Pymm. "Like any grandparent, *Goor* is far more feeble than divine."

"How sad."

"Oh, but there is something that *all* Paranoians do believe in."

"Heavens! What's that?"

"It's *ollagooh*, the essential essence of all living things."

"What a novel idea, 'essential essence,' you say?" cried Ezekiel after a brief lull. "Perhaps this *ollagooh* thing is what's needed here on good old terra firma. It's getting worse all the time, you know. Lord help us, there's even an ad in the

Chronicle on how to purchase a machine gun. All you have to do is send a postcard to ..."

"Not on the air!" shrieked Mulligan.

"P-perhaps that would be unwise," stammered Ezekiel. Then, "As an outside observer, so to speak, do you have any general word of advice for Earth people, something that would help improve our lot?"

"I doo," replied Pymm, suddenly animated. "It is imperative, most imperative, that all of you earthlings — beware the *Mungoliens!*"

A moment of shocked confusion followed, during which time, neither Rufus Mulligan nor Ezekiel immediately responded.

In their view it was obvious that the little blue Paranoian was mad, or simply confused, or had some misconception about the people of Mongolia. My take was that in his study of Earth history, poor Pymm had got his time frame mixed up — and was referring to Mongol Hordes.

"One last question, if I may?" said Ezekiel, the first to recover.

"Do go on, Ezekiel," replied a defeated Rufus Mulligan. "How can it get any worse?"

Fully attentive now, I dreaded what was to follow. In my general view of life, it could always get worse, and usually did.

"Ah yes," replied Ezekiel, with increased zeal. "My sister Phoebe insists that an American by the name of Gattling, invented the machine gun, you know, the 'Gattling gun'? But I've read somewhere that the machine gun was invented by a

Mr. Puckle, who designed his fiendish machine to fire round bullets at Christians and square bullets at Moslems, or..." he hesitated. "Was it the other way around?"

"Go to hell, Ezekiel," bellowed Rufus Mulligan, sucking in an enormous draft of air, nearly doubling in size, "and take your sister with you, and Mr. Puckle, too, and a machine gun for protection, you'll need it, and — and maybe a bottle of *ollagooh*. Bless me, I need a drink."

Ezekiel's line went dead.

"Hee, hee!" chuckled Rufus Mulligan placing his sweaty palms atop his head. "Damn it! They finally got to me. Welcome to Earth, Pymm. That's what earthlings are really like. Oh, oh, the feckless finger points my way. It's time now folks for one last thoughtful word from Adolf Mueller's Chain-Link Fences. If you've got a hankerin' for chain, then — Adolf Mueller's the name."

Mercifully, I blacked out.

Chapter 6 – Mungo Beings

"WHY DOESN'T POOTHY, YOUR *SUUM-MATE*, ever accompany you?" I asked, in the evening of the day following the talk show.

Pymm had once again come rapping on my apartment door and now, perched in the wooden rocking chair, was rocking back and forth contentedly. For some reason he had abandoned his rakish black Fedora.

"Poothy thinks that earthlings are unclean beasts and prefers the solitude of *le saucer*," murmured Pymm, casting sly sylvan looks at the split-leaf philodendron lurking over his shoulder.

"Does Philo upset you, Pymm?" I asked, referring to the plant.

"Philo?"

"Yes, the philodendron. I have a name for all my plants."

"Oh I see, noo. Philo is lonely and I am merely *quarkking* it."

"*Quarkking?*" I breathed.

"Yes, it's a soothing vibrating technique common on Paranoia."
I pointed towards the Venus flytrap plant.

"Can you *quarkk* this shy lady, too?"

Without leaving the sanctuary of his rocking chair, Pymm fixed an icy deep space stare upon the hapless carnivore, holding it a half-dozen seconds or so. Then, to my astonishment, the vice-like jaws began to open and close, open and close, in mute mocking imitation of speech.

"That's hideous!" I cried, unnerved by the gruesome spectacle.

"Sorry, Netherman," murmured Pymm withdrawing his gaze — whereupon the carnivorous creature instantly ceased its bizarre activity.

Still rattled, I hurried into the kitchen and put on the kettle, puttering about the pantry for a moment to settle my nerves.

"Is Paranoia very much different from Earth?" I asked, upon returning to the living room.

Pymm seemed in an expansive philosophic mood — even whilst casting the occasional surreptitious glance at the philodendron.

"Paranoia is a terraqueous planet much like Earth, with mountains, seas, and forests, but noo deserts," he began. "Our atmosphere has a little less oxygen, and I am not quite *this* blue, or any other shade of blue for that matter, on Paranoia," he added, subtly referencing the talk show.

"Speaking of the talk show, Pymm, what was that comment you made about 'beware the Mongolians'? The Mongol hordes swept across Asia almost a thousand years ago."

"Ah, Netherman, I was referring to 'Mungoliens,' not 'Mongolians,' the people from Mongolia, but rather to creatures that originate from a distant corner of the universe, a region known as the Mungo Moon Cluster. It's a moon-like group of planets consisting mainly of rock covered with mysterious surface growths, growths resembling earth mosses, fungi and lichens — and among these mysterious growths dwell the Mungo Beings, or 'Mungoliens' for short."

"Please, let's call them Mungo Beings and not Mungoliens," I suggested. "It's less confusing."

I didn't want to tell Pymm that I had a special fondness for Mongolians, and didn't want to associate any wickedness, or danger, with them, though in fact, the only Mongolian I had ever encountered — and it was only a brief glimpse of him in the lobby — was an older man named Sukh, who lived on the second floor directly above me, and made strange thumping sounds during the night. Apart from that annoyance, which never lasted more than a minute or so, he seemed like a nice old man.

I laughed softly feeling a new sense of intimacy, an intimacy directed towards the little blue man from Paranoia. And Pymm, too, must have shared the feeling, for his words issued forth with a newfound gossamer huskiness — as though he were stroking a favorite pet, or plant.

"I must tell you more about these Mungo Beings, Netherman," he murmured. "They are a most serious threat to the planet Earth."

For an instant I wondered what it would be like to be Pymm's pet, or even plant, but quickly snapped out of it.

There were things I wouldn't tell my psychiatrist, if I had one.

"Please do," I replied solicitously.

"Well then, Mungo Beings are the very tiniest of creatures, yet are intelligent, and wickedly dangerous, and moreover, and I don't wish to alarm you, but they have infested your planet."

"Sorry, Pymm," I snorted, "but that sounds absurd."

"It's a real threat, Netherman. The Mungo Beings first invaded your planet thousands of years ago, and are now deeply embedded among creatures you call 'viruses,' hiding there, if you will."

"Nonsense! That reeks of a ridiculous conspiracy theory. The world abounds with them — and most are about alien incursions."

"Like me? Am I a conspiracy, Netherman?"

"You just could be," I replied, staring back at him brazenly.

"Ah well, maybe if I tell you more about how we first learned of the Mungo Beings, it might help you understand."

"It had better be good, Pymm."

"It is," he replied with a short spasmodic shudder. "Some time ago, *serfs* from the Mungo Moon Cluster were sent to scan Paranoia."

"*Serfs?*"

"Yith, *serfs,* unmanned spaceships."

"Not *saucers?*" I teased.

"No, their spaceships had weird cumbersome-looking shapes, more like giant insects in appearance."

"Sometimes, Pymm," I said softly, "I wonder if any of what you're telling me is true, any of it, or even if you yourself are real."

"Okay, then, why not pinch me?" suggested Pymm.

"Don't be silly," I replied, then without warning I reached over and pinched him on the arm.

"Ouch!" he cried. "That hurt." And after a slight pause, "Are you convinced now?"

"Yeah maybe, but I still think you're paranoid."

"What did you expect, Netherman? I'm a Paranoian. Now, may I continue, it's critical that you should know?"

"If you really want to," I replied.

"Well then, as I was saying, these *serfs* began scanning our planet, with a view to invasion. But we misled them by feeding them information about our lowest life-forms then in a wonderful display of ingenuity, we reverse-engineered their *serf* scans — and learned about the Mungo Beings themselves."

"You turned the tables on them!" I cried.

"Yith, Netherman, we did!" replied Pymm, with unusual vigor. "We are a truly inventive people, but so are the Mungo Beings. Through *their* scans we learned that they had constructed a defensive ring of black holes around the Mungo Moon Cluster, and to manipulate black holes, well, that requires an enormously advanced technology."

"I would certainly think so," I replied.

My own understanding of physics was limited to F = ma, and that bodies attracted each other, which admittedly, I, on occasion, did seriously question — in particular, as it applied to men and women.

At that intriguing moment in our conversation there was a heavy rap on the door. It was the deliveryman with the pescatarian pizza I had ordered prior to Pymm's arrival.

Behind the man loitered the small boy from down the hall.

"Say, mithter, got eny *oig kertins?*" spouted the boy boldly, as I handed the pizza man his money.

"No!" I barked, and grabbing the pizza, slammed the door shut.

"Who was that?" murmured Pymm apprehensively.

"A Mungo Being disguised as a pizza man," I quipped. Pymm glared at me frostily but made no comment. "Are you hungry?" I asked, when I was once again seated. "The pizza's big enough for two."

My mouth had already begun salivating, and I had momentarily banished all thoughts of Mungo Beings and Mungo Moons from my mind.

"Noo," murmured Pymm, and reaching into a well-camouflaged pocket in his suit and withdrawing a small elliptical pouch, he removed a tiny capsule, about the size and appearance of an early June pea, and popped it into his mouth.

"*Bon appétit!*" he declared.

Neither of us spoke for a time, each feasting contentedly in our own-worldly fashion, while outside, a fresh rain beat frenetically against the windowpane.

"Does it rain on Paranoia?" I asked when the pizza was no more.

"Occasionally," murmured Pymm dreamily, his eyes misting over. "Paranoia is like Earth in many ways, but Earth in a distant future, where aggression and barbarism have been suppressed."

"It's a peaceful planet then?"

"Eminently so. It is the final result of natural evolution, when *ollagooh*, our essential essence, finally fully asserts itself."

"Is there any of this *ollagooh* thing in us earthlings?"

Pymm was rocking smoothly back and forth now, apparently quite content — after his nutrient-dot feast.

"I don't know, Netherman. We Paranoians are visiting Earth in pursuit of truth, and whether earthlings possess *ollagooh* is just one of many questions that need answering."

In spite of Pymm's civil manner, and apparent innocence, I could not rid myself of the idea that Pymm's purpose for being on Earth was somehow, more sinister — and not just a quest for truth.

"So all you seek is information?" I asked skeptically.

Pymm hesitated.

"Uh, well … an earthling specimen or two would be nice."

"What?" I cried leaping to my feet, thrusting my face squarely into his. "Care to explain?"

"Ooh! Not many specimens, maybe an earthy for Poothy and an earthy for me," he murmured, sinking deeper into the rocking chair.

"Will you be issuing invitations to these, these earthy specimens, or kidnapping them?" I snorted.

"We would never force anyone against their will," replied Pymm with surprising animation.

Then, an even more alarming thought assailed me!

"You aren't considering me as one of your damn earthling specimens, are you?" I asked.

Pymm uttered a soft fluting laugh.

"Pardon my bluntness, *mon ami*, but you are too unfit to bring back to Paranoia."

And in spite of the obvious insult I was comforted by his words, and sinking back into the softness of the sofa, I relaxed once again. I believed the little blue man. It was more the way he spoke than what he said that convinced me. And a swallow of strong mint tea, with a touch of crème de banane, made me feel even better.

"Not much disease back on Paranoia, is there?" I said chattily, hoping to restore the former atmosphere of *bonhomie*.

"Disease *is* very rare."

"So you people just pop off from old age, eh?"

"Noo," murmured Pymm, "natural death claims only a few, and accidents a few more. Most of us simply self-destruct — dissolve into nothingness when our usefulness is over."

"If usefulness was a criterion for continued life on Earth, then our planet would be uninhabited," I replied cynically.

"I'm becoming increasingly aware of that," replied Pymm softly.

"Tell me, Pymm," I said, brightening up, "there's talk recently here on Earth, that in the future we'll be cloning human beings. Since your culture is so progressive, have you developed any advanced cloning techniques?"

"We doo clone occasionally," replied Pymm, "but it's a very dangerous practice, and consequently, very limited. Most Paranoians are opposed to it though our scientists, at least some of them, persist. The major problem with cloning is the *ollagooh* factor. A clone is never an exact copy of its original, Netherman. The *ollagooh* factor is either missing or highly diminished in the clone."

"The clone has no *ollagooh*!"

"*Exactement!* It does not transfer well in the cloning process."

I restrained a smirk. Pymm seemed to be a cross between a geneticist and an evangelist with his *ollagooh-factor*.

Suddenly, the mood became frosty. Pymm rose stiffly from the rocking chair — reminding me, oddly enough, of a bottle of chilled rosé.

"Poothy and I shall be leaving earth soon," he said coolly.

"I'm sorry to hear that," I grunted, and meaning it. "Is there anything I can do to persuade you to remain a little longer?"

"Noo, Netherman, neither Poothy nor I want to spend one more day on this miserable planet."

"So this is how it ends?"

"Yith, Netherman. It was inevitable."

Awkward and embarrassed, I didn't want Pymm to leave Earth so soon, and so suddenly, but I understood his sentiment.

Ever so abruptly, he bid me a final *adieu* — and not an *au revoir*.

I quickly closed the door behind him to avoid another run-in with the boy from down the hall, my own *oig kertins* — of which there were several — destined for *la poubelle*, as always.

Chapter 7 – In the Valley of the Serpentine

MY HAND HAD BARELY LEFT the doorknob when a wicked idea sprung to mind. *Why not follow the little blue scamp back to his, his saucer?*

I tore out the door after him.

With Pymm gliding smoothly over the pavement ahead of me — indistinguishable from the smattering of other vagabond souls drifting through the streets in the moon-shadowed stillness of the night — I followed stealthily a hundred paces behind.

He never looked back.

As I trudged on, I began to wonder just how Pymm did travel to and from his spaceship. Maybe, just maybe, he had some outlandish way of flying, floating, or simply switching from one place to another.

I dismissed the irksome thought.

He stopped for a red light, forcing me to halt a discrete distance behind. As I stood waiting for the light to change, feeling a little bit awkward, and very lowdown, a warm exhaust-tinted wisp of air stroked my cheek — in mocking imitation of a sultry Mediterranean sea breeze.

The light turned green.

Unconsciously, I stepped forward, and immediately came to a stumbling stop.

Pymm had not moved!

What was the little blue imp up to?

Light after light changed, and still Pymm made no attempt to cross the intersection. A trickle of cars with revving engines and squealing tires, stopped and started, stopped and started, all oblivious to the creature from beyond the Milky Way, poised motionless only a few feet away.

Then a strange sequence of events quickly unfolded.

A powder-blue Chevrolet coupe with fading racing stripes — a scant few oil changes removed from an auto-graveyard — had stopped for a red light.

Pymm sprang forward.

Flinging the passenger door open, he appeared to exchange a few words with the driver, a frizzy-haired youth in a blue-jeans suit, and a moment later, the car — with Pymm planted in the passenger seat — bolted through the intersection.

I watched in utter disbelief.

The little blue scamp was actually hitchhiking!

I ran to a nearby all-night taxi stand.

"There's a sawbuck in it if you keep the Chevy in sight!" I cried to the bald-headed middle-aged driver.

"I am *Polskie*. Whazza sawbuck, pal?" growled the man, with green listless eyes.

In the distance, the Chevy turned onto 152nd Street.

"Here, hurry!" I shouted, thrusting a crumpled ten-dollar bill at him. Disdainfully, he grabbed it, while spitting a tiny projectile lazily out the window.

"*Cholerny!*" he grunted. "It's a slow night. Hop in."

The car lurched forward.

Conversation began immediately.

"You a private eye?"

"Special Operative, Earth Security," I rasped.

"Oh yeah, bill collector, eh?"

"No, it's not quite the same thing," I whispered back.

We turned onto 152nd Street. We were gaining on the Chevrolet.

"Not too close," I warned.

"*Gówno*. I do this before."

"Oh yeah?"

"Yeah, one time this *głupiec* give me a twenty, say 'fooloo thet car,' like some creep in a fuckin' detective movie. I tink he was French."

"What some people expect for twenty bucks," I growled.

"Yeah, I am no *smoczek*. I am *lekarz* back in *Polska*. That mean doctor. Anyway, then, I put on the meter."

During his narrative, the driver periodically drew small seedlike objects from a brown paper bag, chewed them for a while then spat them out the window.

"Then, the meter she run out," he continued, "his twenty bucks, I mean, and he show me his watch, a fuckin' Mickey Mouse watch, with a big fuckin' picture of Mickey Mouse! What'm ah gonna do with a fuckin' Mickey Mouse watch? Cock-sucka!"

Moments passed.

"Maybe you'd better put on the meter," I grunted.

The man laughed.

"Nah, you're okay. Anyway, it's late, business is slow. Say, you know where we go?"

"No," I muttered. "Who knows where an alien will go?"

"Ah! You chase illegal alien?"

I thought for a moment.

Maybe Pymm could be classified as an "illegal alien." The "alien" part was indisputable.

"It's a gray area," I finally replied.

Once again, the driver spat towards the open window. But on this occasion, however, the projectile did not sail harmlessly off into the night like its predecessors, but hovered motionless in a pocket of air, a scant few inches from my face.

I eyed it warily for a second or so, before it sprung at me, glancing off my forehead.

"What'n hell are you chewing?" I snorted.

"Did I git ya?" smiled the driver with bovine innocence. "Sorry, pal, sunflower seeds. My son, he say they good for yah.

He's a fuckin' hippie; vitamins, natural food, that sorta shit. *Gówno!* In my day, it was booze, butts, and broads."

He unconsciously launched another missile into the night.

I wondered briefly over what he had meant by "butts," quickly concluding that he had been referring to cigarette butts.

We left 152nd Street and dropped down into the Valley of the Serpentine, the sinewy Serpentine, more of a swamp than a river. A moon-tinted mist hung low over fields stretching out endlessly on both sides of the road. Each moment, I expected to see a gleaming metallic spaceship poking through the mist, but so far, there was nothing but eerie meadowland.

Then suddenly, up ahead of us, the Chevrolet came to a halt by the side of the road.

"What we do now, eh?" queried the driver.

"Keep going," I shouted, ducking below window level.

Initially, from my crunched position, all I could see was the moonlight glancing off the cabby's white cherubic cheeks. But then as we sped past the parked Chevrolet, his complexion turned beet-red.

"*Chrystus!*" he bleated. "It's a fuckin' Martian! No kiddin', it's a fuckin' blue Martian!"

"You're fuckin' close!" I grunted. "Hey! Stop this thing!"

"Here?" protested the driver, grinding the car to a halt, nonetheless. "You sure, mister, you no see what I see?"

"I'm sure," I said, stepping from the car, and as I started to walk away, the driver stuck his head out the window.

"You know what?" he growled, doltish eyes shining with a new light. "I tink you mix up with bunch of fuckin' Martians, that's what I tink."

"Yeah, you're right, but they're fuckin' Paranoians," I grunted.

The engine rumbled into action, and the taxi throttled away.

Taking a deep breath, I headed back towards the Chevrolet with the faded racing stripes still parked by the side of the road.

Would Pymm emerge, and what would he say if he did? I wondered. But as I was about to reach the Chevy, it suddenly jolted forward, and — making a skidding U-turn in the middle of the road — bolted back in the direction of Linksville, the only head visible, being that of the frizzy-haired driver.

Had Pymm abandoned the vehicle? I wondered, scanning the surrounding mists. But the little blue vamp was nowhere to be seen.

But he had to be somewhere? I thought. *Could he have been hiding in the Chevy as it departed? But why would he do that, come all this way, only to return again? No. He must have ventured down into the surrounding fields, and if that was the case, his spaceship, his "saucer," had to be lurking somewhere nearby, hidden in the mist.*

My pulse quickened.

Fortified by a cocktail of rational thought and grim determination, I plunged boldly through the mist and down a steep embankment — straight into a roadside drainage ditch.

Cursing everything from earthlings to Mungo Beings, I floundered through the cold, darkly veiled water, and up onto the opposite bank. Panting wretchedly, shoes and trousers caked in mire, I slumped to a knee to catch my breath. Wiping away a tear with a shivering finger, I knew I dared not linger in the cold too long.

Struggling to my feet, I began tramping over a meadow-land, soft and spongy from a recent rain, eventually reaching — by dead reckoning — a spot in the field opposite to where the Chevrolet had originally stopped. A cursory inspection of the ground yielded no tracks of any kind apart from mine. Evidently Pymm had not passed this way.

Undaunted, I decided to try the other side of the road.

With haphazard abandon, I plowed back through the drainage ditch, traversed the road, attacked yet a second drainage ditch — they were no longer of any consequence — and took to examining the ground in that region, which to my immense relief, revealed small prim footprints that most assuredly belonged to Pymm.

I whooped with unbridled pleasure.

Swinging both legs easily over the top span of a crooked wooden fence, I entered a muddy expanse of pasture, where-upon, my gum-soled shoes immediately began accumulating huge clumps of mud. Still, I pushed on, like some lead-booted astronaut striding across the surface of some alien planet — while the mist crowded in around me, shimmering in the moonlight, barely illuminating the terrain; the subtle dips and rises, the long deep irrigation ditches, the occasional bundles of compressed hay, along with the ever-present clumps of bent grass.

Did horses still eat hay? I wondered, in this age of pro-cessed food.

Thus preoccupied, I plodded straight into the hind regions of a brown-and-white-spotted Guernsey cow.

Graciously, the tender bovine creature flicked her tail, smiting me on the cheek, warning me to back off. The beast, though undoubtedly startled, did not seem unduly upset, merely mooing softly.

Recoiling in horror, I stumbled backwards, while the well-bred beast hoofed a dignified retreat, the principal effect of the brief encounter being — that I had once again lost Pymm's trail.

Spotting a whitish block about the size and shape of a breadbasket — lying comfortably flat and dry upon a sea of mud — I sat down upon it. Wearily, the fingers of my right hand stroked its sides, then, unconsciously, I pressed a finger to my lips. It had a coarse saline taste, not at all unpleasant.

It was a salt lick set there for the gratification of undoubtedly more of the bovine creatures grazing in the mists!

Suddenly, a sense of futility assailed me, compounded by the weight of my recent spate of blackouts. Weary, muddy, and depressed, tears welled up in my eyes.

"Oh God!" I whimpered. "Why is life such a struggle?"

And at that Job-like moment of crisis, a miracle occurred!

Pymm emerged from the mists, drifting like a vapor, fifty yards away.

I leaped to my feet, misery forgotten, and started after him.

And wonder of all wonders, an instant later, a spaceship appeared, in an immense opening in the mist, and it *was* a shining silver disc, and it was undoubtedly Pymm's *saucer* — lying serenely in the middle of a cow pasture. Two-hundred yards away, it glowed with an ethereal brightness that melted away the surrounding mist.

I fell to my knees, trembling with the reverence of it all.

Recovering quickly, I rose to my feet. Pymm was now far ahead of me, zigzagging through the soft pastureland.

Did I dare follow after him? I wondered, but only for an instant. *Of course, I did!*

The *Second Crossing* shone too brightly to gaze upon directly — even the reflection off the meadow proved harsh — so I adopted the tactic of taking ten steps forward, eyes firmly shut, pausing for a quick glimpse of the spaceship for direction, then taking ten more steps, and in thus fashion, crept forward. Finally, during one of these pauses, I caught a fleeting glimpse of Pymm's pencil-like form vanishing into the spaceship's sphere of light.

What would he say when he saw me? I wondered, trembling with anticipation. *Surely, he would welcome me, civilly at least, if not warmly. After all, he had come "a knocking uninvited on my front door" — as ominously as any raven.*

Suddenly, an utterly terrifying thought weaseled into my consciousness.

What if the entire sequence of events that night had all been part of a sinister plot to lure me to the spaceship? And was that Pymm's plan, a devilish plan to take me captive, transport me back to Paranoia with him — as one of his damn earthling specimens?

I forced the gruesome thought from my mind.

Moments later, a momentary spell of dizziness caused me to sway. The physical exertions of the night were more than I was accustomed to, so a little dizziness was nothing to be alarmed at, even expected.

I pushed gallantly on.

Then suddenly, I was on my knees, doubled over in agony, my stomach an aching knotted ball, pierced by sporadic splinters of pain.

What could it be, I wondered, in anguish — *a stomach ache, something I had eaten?*

The crouching seemed to help, however, and a few minutes later, I was back on my feet, and on my way again, thankful that my distress had only been a fleeting thing. With renewed determination, I waved a clenched fist at the spaceship, so tantalizingly close now.

An instant later, I was back on my knees again, this time with pain so severe, that I could not scream, though I desperately wanted to.

It was a long, long time before the pain subsided, and when it did, I found myself drenched from head to toe in perspiration, lying on the ground, utterly exhausted. Finally, when able to, I rose to my feet and glared balefully at the spaceship.

Was the agony I had just experienced due to the "alien-shield" that Pymm had referred to on his first visit to my apartment?

On a gut-impulse, I took one last stubborn testing step forward, in the direction of the spaceship. Searing stabs of pain instantly hammered me backwards, a bestial scream escaping my lungs, just before I blacked out. When I came to, hours later it seemed, the mist had cleared, the moon had vanished from above — but the spaceship still remained, roosting in the pasture like some contented silver alien bird of prey. I struggled to my feet — and giving the spaceship one long, lasting intense stare — started the long trek home.

Why did aliens have to be so damn difficult? I wondered.

Chapter 8 – A Pink Fit

"IT'S YOU, PYMM!" I CRIED breathlessly, as I opened the door.

"I knoow," murmured Pymm, clearly distraught — his chest bellowing in and out alarmingly.

"Inside, quick!" I urged, glancing nervously down the hallway.

"Why, Netherman?" whispered Pymm, ducking under my arm.

"Reporters," I grumbled. "They've been a damn nuisance."

Probably as a consequence of the talk show, my address had been leaked to the press, and as a result, my modest apartment had been besieged with reporters and visitors — everyone wanting to meet and talk to the Man from Paranoia. As a last resort, I had switched the number on my front door with that of a nearby apartment, and for the time being, the stratagem appeared to be working.

"What irks you, my little alien friend?" I asked endearingly.

I had accepted the possibility of never seeing Pymm again, but was delighted at his reappearance. Yet, instinctively, I decided not to tell him of my venture into the Valley of the Serpentine the previous evening.

"Noothing," moaned Pymm.

"Noothing's bothering you?" I mocked.

"Oh, well, if I must," sighed Pymm, as he fluttered into the rocking chair like a crazed butterfly — causing the giant philodendron with the broad groping leaves to shrink into its corner.

"Look what you're doing, Pymm!" I shrieked. "You're terrorizing my dear plants."

The tendrils on the ring of snake plants were shivering hideously, and the poor miniature yucca plant had keeled over, unexpectedly, and lay rigidly supine upon the sandy soil.

"Soo sorry, Netherman, I've been selfishly thoughtless," he soughed, his skin — normally bluish, of course — having taken on an alarming silvery-pink deathly cast. "It's the news I bear."

"Has it anything to do with Mungo Beings?" I teased.

"Noo," he murmured, his frosty pupils flaring for an instant. "But I'm warning you, Netherman. They quietly wait, building up their armies, and soon, they will attack."

"Thank God for that," I replied, then realizing my mistake, added, "What I mean, Pymm, is, thank God for the delay. Now then, what is it that's bothering you?"

"I-I suppose I'm having a pink fit, I suppose I really am," he replied, slumping deep into the hump of the rocking chair.

I gulped.

"You do look a bit pinkish."

"I'm not supposed to."

"Is it contagious?"

"Noo," murmured Pymm mournfully. "It's just a wretched feeling of melancholy when everything seems hopeless."

"A down-in-the-dumps sort of thing?" I offered.

"Yith."

"We call it 'having the blues,'" I sighed.

"How quaint!" replied Pymm, his eyes sparkling for an instant.

Feeling somewhat "bluesy" myself I went to the record player and put on a Nina Simone single, and with the throaty thrumming refrain of "What's the matter daddy, come on, save my soul, I need some sugar in my bowl," I went into the kitchen and put on the kettle.

Minutes later I returned to the living room pleased to discover that the plants had quieted down, and mercifully, too, Pymm had managed to control his emotions somewhat better. With Simone now faintly lilting in the background, Pymm eyed me, balefully, as I gently poured the tea into my delicate Bulgarian teacups.

"You have a knack for making tea," he murmured sociably.

"Oh, it's nothing special," I replied modestly, "just mint, with a blend of ginger and honey, and occasionally a dab of *crème de banane*."

"Nice mixture," he warbled.

"Out with it, Pymm!" I snapped, unable to stand it any longer. "You've stalled long enough."

"Okay, Netherman, I suppose I must share my misfortune with you," replied Pymm, draining the piping hot tea without wincing. "It's just that — our *orgasm* has developed a malfunction."

"Our *orgasm*?" I asked, bewildered. "Do *we* have an *orgasm*?"

"I mean the *Second Crossing's orgasm*."

"Is it a serious malfunction?"

"Of course," he crackled. "Why else a pink fit?"

"What will you do?"

"I dunoo," he moaned, "without a perfectly functioning *orgasm* — the big thrust needed to reach Paranoia is impossible."

"You'll get to like it here on Earth, Pymm," I whispered devilishly. "It grows on people. All earth-babies don't like Earth when they're born. That's why they cry, but they soon get used to it."

"I'm not an earth-baby!" replied Pymm peevishly. "I fear that poor Poothy and I will perish here. Still, there is one small hope."

"Which is?"

"Well, as it happens, the *First Crossing* still remains buried in the desert in Nevada," he replied, his cut-stone eyes glistening with new determination. "Its *orgasm* might still be functional."

"So, why not go to Nevada and check it out?"

"That's the problem, Netherman. Without help, the *Second Crossing* might not be able to reach Nevada."

And then I thought to myself. Yes, the First Crossing *had been buried in the Nevada desert, but I suspected that — since several days had passed since its arrival — it had to have been found by the U.S. authorities. After initially sighting the alien craft, particularly an alien craft that had actually landed on Earth — and one with a particularly unique defense — they would have persisted, and returned to the site, and possibly, even probably, detected its presence there, buried in the sand — using some powerful form of metal-detector.*

And by now, it had most likely been taken away to some secret laboratory — perhaps under the flanks of Mount Rushmore — and been inspected, prosected, exsected, photographed, x-rayed, microscoped, laser-beamed, and very possibly, Turtle-Waxed.

No, that was one saucer Pymm would never see again!

"We musht doo something," continued Pymm, shuddering in appalling fashion, slurring his words. "Musht look, musht look, and you musht, too, Netherman. You musht come with us to Nevada."

"Good luck with that!" I replied defiantly. "I'm not going anywhere with you, Pymm."

My nightmare of being on Paranoia, in that weird hospital — Ataraxia, was it not? — still haunted me. And though I felt endeared towards Pymm, I also was wary of him.

Then teasingly, I added: "What do you think caused the malfunction in your spaceship, Pymm? Could it have been those Mungo Beings, those Mungoliens?"

"Ab-ab-ab-surd!" jabbered Pymm, highly agitated.

A Paranoian pink fit was something to behold!

"Yes, yes, sorry, Pymm," I hastened to reply. "That was a poor joke, a poor joke. It couldn't have been Mungo Beings."

"Noo, noo," hooted Pymm, "they're too small."

The telephone rang, suddenly, jarringly. I lifted the receiver an inch then dropped it. Hopefully, the caller would take the hint.

"Help us, Netherman," pleaded Pymm. "The *orgasm* is soo weak. We need your help to get to Nevada."

What help could I possibly offer? I wondered. *And though I was touched by his entreaty, and his terrible anguish — there was no way I would venture with him to Nevada.*

"I'm not going anywhere in your *saucer*," I finally declared.

"Why not?" quivered Pymm. "It's a short journey."

"It's a short journey to Paranoia, too, so I gather."

Then, for no apparent reason, Pymm's pink fit suddenly vanished. One moment he had been brooding and cloyingly pleading, and the next, normal — in so far as any Paranoian could be normal — and once again, he was rocking back and forth contentedly in the rocking chair.

"Why such an aversion to traveling in *le saucer*, Netherman?" he asked, his voice gently crackling — with a new magnetic quality that seemed to reach out and grip me. "And why are you so afraid of Paranoia? Are you not curious? Consider it for a moment my earthling friend. Ponder a place beyond the sun, beyond the Milky Way, another galaxy. Doesn't that stir you?" His voice grew even more vibrant. "Envision a culture, infinitely refined, infinitely faceted, and so very sensuously pleasing. Doesn't that tempt you? Don't all you earthlings dream of such a thing?"

Then a dim thought corkscrewed into my consciousness.

Was Pymm attempting to quarrk me?

"I-I certainly have no idea what other earthlings dream of, Pymm," I blurted out. Huge tears began welling up in my eyes. "You think that we're barbarians, that television's bad, and talk shows, too, and uh … that the Earth has too much sand." The tears were now cascading freely down my cheeks. "But I happen to like television, and talk shows, and even sand. An earthling's life is short, Pymm. All I've ever done of any consequence is write a few simple novels, very simple novels, but I've tried, tried hard, and my life might not seem like much to you, but I don't want to change it." I blew my nose, fiercely, into a dinner napkin. "I won't leave Earth, not now, not ever!"

And with that, the rant ended, and I, too, was calm again.

"As you wish, *mon vieux*," murmured Pymm.

Taking a deep breath, I carefully scrutinized the little blue man, and came to a decision, a decision that shocked even me.

"I will go with you to Nevada," I said finally, in a determined voice, "and help you if I can, but promise me that there'll be no treachery?"

"You have my word, as a Paranoian," murmured Pymm.

Perhaps it was naive of me, but as an earthling, I believed him.

Chapter 9 – The Sensuum

WE WALKED A CROOKED PATH through a meadowland dry and firm — there not having been rain in over twenty-four hours. A faint luminescent mist streaked the crisp night air. With a heart beating double-time, I sighted the *Second Crossing* glowing splendidly in its quilt of darkness, and shivered involuntarily, for tonight — I was destined to board her!

"Why did you pick this spot to land in?" I asked wonderingly.

"Poothy likes cows," replied Pymm tersely.

"Cows?"

"Yith, there are no cows on Paranoia."

"Oh," I replied, wary of pursuing the topic.

Fifty yards from the spaceship, I broke out into a heavy sweat.

"There will be no discomfiture tonight, *mon ami*," murmured Pymm, sounding uncomfortably like Charles Boyer. "The alien-shield has been turned off."

"You knew about me following you the other night?" I grunted.

"Of course, Netherman. Poothy was watching you on the scan. Frankly, Earth bores her beyond belief. Her only relief are the antics of earthlings attempting to approach *le saucer* using jeeps, helicopters, hang-gliders, motorcycles, and even tricycles."

"Tricycles?"

"Yith. There was one toddling boy on a child's three-wheeler."

"And Poothy zapped him?"

"Yith. With much delight," murmured Pymm.

"But where are all these people now?" I asked, mystified. We had not seen a single soul *en route*.

"The incursions seemed to have stopped. Don't ask me to interpret earthlings' behavior, Netherman, I'm new here."

An open portal beckoned.

Numb with misgiving, I stepped inside — and was immediately seized by what only can be described as a field, an invisible force field, that made every muscle, bone, and sinew in my body quiver.

"Do not worry, Netherman," murmured Pymm calmly. "The quiet oscillations you feel stimulate inter-cellular transfer, and are a natural aid to our biochemical processes. It's an ancient idea. Everything vibrates on Paranoia, even the planet itself."

"Have we taken off, yet?" I breathed, attempting to peer into the blurry interior of the spaceship.

"Yith, we left Earth as soon as the portal closed," intoned Pymm.

"Oh no! You haven't tricked me, have you?" I cried, with a sudden panic. "We're not going to Paranoia are we?"

"Relax, Netherman," murmured Pymm. "We've merely lifted off the ground and will be heading for Nevada, as I told you we would."

A strange hissing sound sifted through the silvery gray shadows, chilling me to the bone.

Was it a voice? No, it couldn't be, it was too ephemeral.

The sound slowly became more distinct, and incredibly enough, it was a voice, slurred and sinister.

"Pymms! Why did you bring the earthling here?" it scolded.

"Be civil!" chided Pymm sharply.

"But the creature's soo uncouth?" challenged the voice.

I listened, mute and immobile.

"It's just, Netherman, Poothy — the earthling I told you about. He has agreed to help us reach the *First Crossing.* Shed your natural inclination and be civil. *Goor* knows, I had to," chastised Pymm.

"*Goor?*" I whispered. "Is this the *Goor* you mentioned on the talk show?"

"Yith, the giver and the spreader of *ollagooh,* according to some."

"But not you?"

"Noo, though I do occasionally invoke the name. It's ingrained in our speech much like 'God' is in yours."

And while Pymm and I were having our subtle metaphysical discussion — Poothy materialized from out of the shadows.

To my astonishment, she was not a fecund replica of Pymm, which I confess I had grown to expect, but was taller than Pymm by almost three hands — I had gotten rather comfortable with reckoning Paranoian heights using hands — and rakishly slight, like a child. Although she wore a thin shimmering translucent outfit covering certain parts of her body — like Pymm, though more visible — her skin underneath was a dark, heavily mottled blue, and remarkably scale-like in texture, unlike Pymm's. Her chest was boyishly flat, still there was an unmistakable air of femininity about her, and in her haughty serpentine fashion, she was, admittedly, strikingly seductive.

I attempted to mask my natural physical inclination, but was hopelessly unable to do so.

"I will *decontam* him at once," whispered Poothy chillingly.

Pymm, his gray eyes shining approvingly, faded into the shadows.

"Wait, w-wait!" I cried out in desperation. "Please, w-wait!" But it was too late. I was alone with Poothy — and utterly terrified.

"Remove your cloth," she hissed imperiously.

"I won't," I grunted defiantly.

"How peculiar! Why not?"

"It's not d-done on Earth."

She gasped.

"You mean earthlings never remove their cloth?"

"N-no, not that," I explained, with a growing feeling of helplessness. "It's just that a man doesn't undress in front of a strange woman."

"I am *not* strange," she sniffed, mildly pouting.

"I-I didn't mean that," I replied.

"Perhaps not, but you *are* peculiar. How does Pymms stand you?"

I muttered something incomprehensible.

Poothy laughed, a wicked susurration — sending shivers up my spine. Then she slid towards me, and to my utter astonishment, in an instant, every thread of clothing I had borne lay in a loose mound at my feet.

There was no magical or mystical explanation for what had happened. She had simply moved with remarkable swiftness, and unerring deftness, and, of course — she had caught me unawares.

In total shock, I stood trembling, awkward and naked, before her.

And before I could recover, she was upon me once again, this time, wielding a grotesque object with wiggling arms and wobbling green sponges — vaguely resembling a mass of tiny wriggling octopuses.

I nearly shed my skin in terror as she pressed the unearthly device against me. The sponges clung, hissed, and sucked as they crept slowly over my body, each sponge poising hypnotically for an instant above each bodily nook and cranny before moving on.

I suppressed a scream, then found myself laughing hysterically, with the realization that the strange device was nothing more than a vacuum cleaner — a bizarre Paranoian vacuum cleaner.

"Don't squirm, creature!" she cried. "It's only an *octopore.*"

"I'm no creature," I snorted, but I did submit to the groping, which was, admittedly, becoming increasingly more pleasurable.

"It's not perfect *poring,* mind you," hissed Poothy, "but for an earthling, what can one expect?" Then in a higher pitched voice, and with a hint of dread, she added, "You aren't coming to Paranoia, are you?"

"Not if I can help it," I sighed, reveling in my senses.

"Thank *Goor* for that."

Too soon, the *poring* ended, and Poothy ushered me into a tightly confining chamber where a pungent vitriolic spray pummeled my helpless body from every conceivable suffocating direction. Mercifully, the ordeal lasted but a minute, and after an even briefer sojourn — in some kind of drying device that she referred to as a *woven* — I was handed a pink dressing gown with a texture softer than fleece.

By now I was feeling wonderfully exhilarated — and even looking forward to Poothy's next offering.

"Come noow, come with me, into the *sensuum,*" slurred Poothy.

Obediently, I followed the slinky enchantress into an odd, elegantly vague room with no apparent walls, ceiling, or floor. There were no details for the eye to settle upon, no fixture, ornament, or item of furniture, nothing, just a soft, inviting cushion of grayness.

Instinctively my knees buckled, and I fell backward, reclining in the grayness. Poothy, her shimmering outfit inexplicably gone, lay beside me, tugging at my dressing gown, whispering mockingly in my ear.

"Earthy, earthy creature, breathe softly, deep and softly."

My dressing gown slipped away.

"What's going on?" I muttered feebly.

"Do not speak!" hissed Poothy imperiously, "for the sake of all that's pure, do not speak. Lie back. Allow your limbs to lighten, your mind to drift. You have a mission to perform, a mission to perform."

Mission? I thought dreamily.

Barely cognizant of her words, though certainly not her presence, I lay back compliantly — letting the sinews of my body yield their last remaining pockets of tension.

"Lovely, lovely Earth creature," sighed Poothy.

"I'm not a creature, not a creature, not a creature," I heard my own voice repeat, as it receded into the background.

I lay there supine for an unknown interval of time, staring bemusedly into oblivion, then slowly came the awareness, that not every part of my anatomy had, in fact, relaxed. One region, in particular, an annexation of my body — with a rebellious inclination of its own — had stiffened notably. Raising my head, and peering timorously downwards — my eyeballs nearly sprung from their sockets, as they focused upon an enormously swollen penis.

That couldn't possibly be me? was my first thought, but of course, it had to be. A hasty glance at Poothy reassured me that she, at least, was not gaping rudely at me.

Then with a newfound surge of pride, I surreptitiously let my fingertips tenderly probe its surface — in an innocent expression of curiosity.

"You are so deliciously peculiar!" murmured Poothy.

She had turned in my direction, and was extending a thin bamboo finger towards my face, a finger coated with a strange brown paste.

"Sweet creature, press this to your lips."

I shrank back, but the persistent wench reached out towards me with an inescapably long tentacle arm, and touched the substance to my lips —which to my great surprise, had the taste of peanut butter, and was seemingly entirely harmless.

"A Paranoian brand, no doubt," I tittered foolishly.

"Do not s-speak!" hissed Poothy, with a flare of anger, but recovering quickly enough. "Droop down into fantasy, into desire, into lussht — especially lussht. Droop down into deep earthly lussht!"

What was this "lussht" the foolish woman was prattling on about? I wondered innocently enough.

But, in the interest of good fellowship, and interplanetary relations, I did as she advised, and soon found myself fantasizing, not about voluptuous blondes with bulging breasts and curving thighs, but oddly enough, about Poothy herself. Mentally, dreamily, I slowly explored the surface of her mottled blue shivering torso.

Then with a bold, enterprising pounce, she was upon me, her hot sultry breath wafting against my loins, as brazenly, she seized my very codpiece, and began stroking it with skillful, scaled fingertips. Unrelentingly, she teased it, repeatedly, with her flickering reptilian tongue, until finally her full moist lips engulfed it totally, suckling it so sweetly, so tenderly, that every pore in it strove to fill the gentle cup.

I squirmed in ecstasy.

"Lovely, lovely, though undeniably peculiar, earthling creature," she whimpered, surfacing for air.

Then she fell upon me once again, while I in turn — cerebrally, at least — ravished every inch of her lithe, sinewy body.

We lay enmeshed — for an eternity, or so it seemed.

"Eternity" ended rather abruptly, when my besieged member sprang free from its tender enslavement — thrusting upwards like a rocket ship, ready for blastoff. Torrents of laughter bubbled up inside me.

How ludicrous! That, that thing, that throbbing tentacular thing, that beating bowsprit, that mutinous galactic growth could not possibly be attached to me.

Then without warning, I shrieked with pleasure as a tremendous seminal stream shot high into the air, forming a long iridescent arc disappearing into the surrounding grayness.

And there was Poothy hovering above me once again, her slender hips swaying from side to side, suggestively, her gemstone eyes piercing my very soul. With indescribable pain, I reached out for her, and drew her to me, and assaulted her — in glorious earthly missionary fashion.

After the frenzy, I sank into a languid semi-consciousness — and lingered there for an indeterminable interval of time.

Then Pymm materialized from out of the grayness.

"We have a problem, Netherman," he muttered gloomily.

"What kind of a problem?" I asked dizzily.

"It concerns the *First Crossing*."

"What about it? Are we in Nevada already?"

"Yith, Netherman. It was a remarkably quick jump."

Chapter 10 – Old Mundy

I STOOD ON THE COARSE salt-sand staring off into the distance, the only break in a desert landscape of saguaro cacti, mesquite trees, and palo verde bushes, being a foreboding shadowy region of black rocks five hundred yards away. Closer at hand, a flock of tumbleweeds struggled to free themselves from a clump of living sagebrush.

Pymm stood by my side gazing pensively into the depths of a shallow irregular crater. Poothy — for personal reasons — had remained inside the *Second Crossing* roosting nearby.

"Where are we, Pymm, exactly?" I muttered, breaking the desert stillness. "How far away is the nearest town?"

"Far away, Netherman, far, far away," murmured Pymm.

The *Second Crossing* had managed to reach Nevada safely, but we now faced a major problem. Its scanner had located the *First Crossing* buried deep under the sand — its only marker being that small jagged crater. But the question remained: Was the *Second Crossing's orgasm* strong enough to pull it out?

Pymm didn't think so.

Although the *orgasm* had had enough "juice" to reach Nevada, it was nowhere near fully restored. We were stymied, behind the eight ball — screwed, as some would say — or, at least, Pymm was.

The squeal of a hawk circling high overhead punctuated the gravity of the situation.

"Let's face it, Pymm," I said soberly, "we need help to dig it out. We should contact the authorities."

"Noo, Netherman, noo more earthlings," moaned Pymm, savagely kicking at a passing tumbleweed and missing. "We will use the last remaining strength of the *Second Crossing's orgasm* to try to lift it out. If we fail — I fear that Poothy and I are doomed to remain on this barbarous planet forever."

"Easy, Pymm, easy," I replied.

The little blue man's manners were beginning to irritate me. Yes, Earth was in some ways an iniquitous planet, but he didn't have to be so blunt about it.

The wind picked up and began shifting the sand, back and forth, back and forth, the desolate desecrating sand that appeared ready to swallow us up — reminding me, oddly enough, of an *avant-garde* movie I seemed to recall having seen, in some "art's theater" years ago.

I remembered the movie, mainly because of the number of vagrants in trench coats inside the theater — slinked down in their seats, watching the movie with their eyes closed, hands deep within their pockets.

I had been told to ignore them by the ticket seller.

"Why?" I had asked.

"They have holes in the pockets of their coats," he had explained.

"So?" I had responded.

He gave me a "Who is this guy?" look, handing me my ticket.

I had watched the movie with both hands firmly planted on the back of the seat in front of me.

The movie itself involved a primitive tribe of yellow-striped natives, living in pits dug deep into the sand. Because of their dry environment, they were compelled to make long, arduous treks across the sand to a distant river for life-preserving water. This had been the custom for time immemorial.

Then one day, a scholar happened by, a disillusioned young city man wandering the remote regions of the earth in a quest for "truth." The youth was immediately beset upon by the natives and dumped into a pit in the sand — along with a tribe elder's unwed daughter. The scholar tried, repeatedly, to scale the walls of the pit and escape, but the sand kept crumbling under his fingertips, then later, whilst he slept, the yellow-striped men would climb down into the pit on knotted ropes, and rebuild the walls.

As the days passed it became evident that the young man was to be kept prisoner, indefinitely, and that the native girl was to be his mate. Finally, in time, the young man succumbed to the inevitable amorous entanglement with the maiden, and with it, tacit membership in the tribe. And still, the youth continued to remain a prisoner in the pit, dug deep into the sand.

Not long after his conversion, however, the scholar made a startling discovery, one that contributed, in the profoundest way, to the general well-being of the tribe.

The young man's analytical mind had reasoned that sand, no matter how dry, must nevertheless contain some water, even if only in the most minute quantities. With this simple idea in mind, he buried a bucket in the sand, a bucket with its open end tightly sealed by a stout porous cloth. And miraculously, only a few days later, the bucket was retrieved almost a quarter filled with cold, clear water.

This fortuitous discovery meant that the natives no longer had to make long, arduous journeys to the distant river, but could draw water from the life-giving sand itself.

The youthful scholar was hailed, gloriously, and showered with gifts, everything from fossilized cockleshells to turquoise inlaid silver rings, yet still — he remained a prisoner in the pit dug deep into the sand.

They were a simple people — those yellow-striped natives — but not naive. And as it happened, the wandering scholar spent the rest of his natural life, with the woman in the pit, dug deep into the sand.

"Heigh! Hol'up a min't," crackled a throaty voice behind us.

Spinning around, I espied a rickety old man trundling across the sand towards us, a man coated from head to foot — in what appeared to be soot!

"Might glad ah ketch't youse fellers 'fore youse hop't thet flyin' saucer. Thet's wha' 'tis, ain't it?" he said, spitting out the words.

"It's *un saucer*, yith," murmured Pymm amicably.

But I was not as amicably inclined as my Paranoian friend. For one thing, the man was a stranger, and for another — the man had frightened the innards out of me.

"Where'n hell did you come from?" I demanded.

The blackened face crinkled into a smile.

"Bin hol't up'n them rocks yonder," he jawed, spitting in the direction of the black rocks, black-rimmed eyeballs rolling menacingly. "Kin youse fellers oblige me wif'n what yer doin' 'roun here?"

"We're here on a strictly confidential matter, a matter of some delicacy, government business, top secret stuff," I replied, motioning for Pymm to remain silent, our business in the desert being too sensitive in nature, too off-ball to involve the old man — though he himself seemed something of an "off-ball." "It might be in your best interest to tell us what *you're* doing here?"

"Spit on muh butt," gummed the old man. "Youse sure 're a mealy-mouth't snip, ain't youse? Wha' d'youse think ah'm doin' middle a the dissert? This here's muh home. Ah'm a prospecter." And with a broad, toothless grin, he extended his hand. "Old Mundy's muh handle."

"I'm Netherman," I replied, reluctantly accepting the handshake.

"Youse a commie?"

"Of course not," I snorted. "This is my friend, Pymm," —
adding as an afterthought, "he's not a commie either."

"Looks kinda blue, don' he. Bin holdin' his breath a might
too long?" jawed Old Mundy, before howling gleefully.

"Brace yourself, old fellow," I warned. "Pymm here is, in
fact, a creature from another planet."

"Thet so?" quipped Old Mundy.

"Yip, thet's so," I mocked.

"One a them blue critters, them Per'noy'ns, eh? Why ah
thought they'd all a skeedaddle't outta here by now."

"You know about them?" I gasped.

"Shore do!" exclaimed Old Mundy, with a sly coyote grin.
"Ah wuz witness tuh both a thir landin's."

"You witnessed the arrival of the *First Crossing*?" asked
Pymm, stiffening noticeably.

"Shore did, more'n a week back," replied the old prospector.

He stood for a moment eyeing us critically — his jaws
working feverishly on some mysterious substance.

"Well?" I said impatiently. "Go on, out with it!"

Old Mundy scowled.

"Please, sir, would you kindly tell us your tale?" murmured
Pymm respectfully, displaying a remarkable social adaptability.

"Wahl then, since youse're askin' kindly," replied Old
Mundy. "Now less see. The firs' time ah witness't a saucer
landin', thir wuz this coyote moon a bearin' down from above,
sneaky like, wif'n jess 'nough light so's youse could step on a
rattler wif'n out knowin' it. Then sudden like, out of nowhir,
thir wuz sech a awful blaze a light — like the sun'd popp't back

inter the sky. Lordy! Ah fell tuh muh knees en confess't muh sins right thir on the spot, keepin' muh eyelids shut tight as a gopher's bite — en whin ah open't 'em, Crissy me! Thir wuz this flyin' saucer a sittin' thir, so nice en purty, jess like thet one." For emphasis, Old Mundy hurled an enormous wad of spittle in the direction of the *Second Crossing*. "En 'fore ah know't, a little blue critter wuz struttin' t'werds me. Lordy me! Ain't fraid tuh say it folks, but — ah wuz shittin' like a mule."

"He must have been the 'sand creature' that Broom encountered," I quietly whispered to Pymm.

"Most likely," replied Pymm, and then addressing Old Mundy, tension in his voice. "Would you please describe the 'little blue critter' that you saw? Did he have an ovate cranium, a notched ear lobe, and a recessed zygomatic arch?"

"Tarnation!" screeched Old Mundy. "Ah tol' youse. He wuz a short, skinny blue feller."

"What happened next?" I asked, not only annoyed at the tiresome old codger, but also, captivated by his tale.

"Wahl, ah jess skedaddle't outta thir."

"You said that that was the first time you saw a flying saucer land," I said. "So you were also witness to a second landing?"

"Yip. Two nights later the same thin' happened. The saucer lant't in the same spot. Ah wuz wonderin' if it would return en Lordy be, it daid. This time ah had on a clean pair a britches en ah intent't tuh keep 'em thet way. But jumpin' jackrabbits, this time thir wuz two a them li'l blue critters — struttin' t'werds me like a pair a buzzerts."

"That must have been Broom and Elsymm," murmured Pymm, his voice dripping with emotion.

"Go on," I muttered.

"Wahl, shucks!" replied Old Mundy scratching his brow thoughtfully. "Tuh muh great surprise, they greet't me like ah wuz the guv'ner a Nevady — which sly dog thet ah is, ah tol' 'em ah wuz."

"And then?" I asked breathlessly.

"Truth be tol'," replied Old Mundy, grinning like a buzzard, "ah show't 'em genuin' dissert hospitoolity en invit't them critters inter town fer a drink."

"Town?" I grunted, staring hard at the old recluse, wondering if he was as sun-baked as he appeared. "What town? There isn't a town within a hundred miles of here."

"Y'ain't from 'roun' here are youse, mister?" chided Old Mundy, his jaw twitching alarmingly. "So youse kin kindly keep yer dumb 'pinions tuh yerself."

"Why you old buzzard!" I snarled, feeling the blood rushing to my face. "Show me a town and I'll, I'll..." The old codger's foul garments caught my eye. "I'll trade what I'm wearing for your stinking outfit, soot and all."

"Youse got yerself a deal, sonny," replied Old Mundy scornfully, his neck bobbing up and down like a vulture's. "This way gents. Foller me — en don' look't thuh san'."

Chapter 11 – Rattler Gulch

WHY OLD MUNDY HAD SAID "Don' look't the san'" I could not fathom, especially since he had also, later, warned us to "Keep a eye peel't fer rattlers." Nevertheless, we proceeded without much ado, first bypassing the black rocks where Old Mundy had "hol't up," then continuing on for an additional mile or so, across a desert sand sometimes soft and yielding like dry table salt, but oftentimes hard and crusty like frozen tundra. Pymm straggled in the rear, mesmerized by the sand, kicking at it and even occasionally bending down and sifting it in his hands.

Eventually we reached the start of an arroyo, whose naturally curving course we followed for yet another mile, until finally, we stumbled into a row of half-buried wind-torn ancient shacks.

A sun-bleached signpost read: RATTLER GULCH – WELCOME ALL RATTLERS EN VARMINTS.

Unfortunately, for me, I had to admit, it was indeed a town and I had lost my wager.

"We got us some swappin' tuh do," chorused Old Mundy, fumbling with the thin rope supporting his breaches.

We traded clothing in the middle of Rattler Gulch's main street — witnessed by the gaping wooden facades of a bygone era. Outfitted in my stylish brown corduroy suit, Old Mundy proudly pranced about the soulless street with long, exaggerated strides, eventually stopping at the battered door of the "liv'ry stable."

Out of curiosity, I poked my head inside the door — hanging precariously by a single hinge.

"I don't see any horses," I muttered, absentmindedly — to no one in particular, something I did from time to time, a consequence of being a recluse. "Just some harnesses, covered in dust and a busted carriage with an ornate grill."

"Jumpin' jackrabbits!" exclaimed Old Mundy. "Thir ain't bin a horse 'n Rattler Gulch fer more'n a hunnert years."

I laughed easily.

Old Mundy's unrelentingly uncouth manner no longer bothered me. On the long trek into town, I had come to the rational conclusion that the only way to deal with the cantankerous old fool was to ignore him, as much as possible.

We stood before a broad wooden building with the faded word "*LOON*" inscribed upon the façade.

"This here's where ah hitches muh britches whin ah ain't loan't 'em tuh some jackass," jawed Old Mundy, shuffling through the swinging doors.

The saloon was a fossil, just like the old coot. A high wooden bar, and a rickety staircase leading to a narrow balcony, crowded in upon a small drinking area cluttered with circular wooden tables and rough-hewn wooden chairs. Behind the bar stretched a long, horizontal mirror with an intricately carved fringe. To the left of the mirror was a faded poster announcing the impending arrival of Lillie Langtry, Jersey Lily — "a gal with talent, temperament, and a tantalizing torso."

Included in her proffered program was "a recitation from the works of Oscar Wilde, numerous free-spirited and personal anecdotes drawn from London's high society, and free photographic images to the first forty patrons to purchase a ticket." A rectangle, approximately six inches by eight, had been torn out of the center of the poster where Lillie Langtry's image most likely had been.

To the right of the mirror, mounted in brass fittings, was a double-barreled shotgun of antique vintage. Despite all expectation, the hall appeared to be remarkably dust and sand free.

"Where is everyone?" I muttered unthinkingly.

"Feedin' the buzzerts, yuh dumb fuss-bucket!" gummed Old Mundy. "This here's a ghos' town," and with his chest puffed out like a rooster's, he drew a bottle from behind the bar. "Bein' the sole resident, en con'squently, mayor, preacher en barkeep, has its 'vanterges," he declared with a malicious grin.

It occurred to me, suddenly, almost in a dream, that Old Mundy might easily be the cross between a lonely desert hermit and some unfortunate wayward coyote, because of the peculiar way that his nose and chin thrust outward, converging to form a snout. It wasn't a flattering image of the man, but it was comforting to me.

We stood at the bar facing the mirror — and consequently, somewhat disconcertingly, staring at each other through it. Old Mundy lined up three shot glasses, filling them to the brim with whiskey.

"Yer health, gents," he grunted, downing his in one easy motion.

I followed suit, surprised at how smooth the liquid was.

"How do you like living here?" I asked, enjoying the buzz.

"Wahl, it's kinda peaceful like," drawled Old Mundy contentedly, then noticing that Pymm had not touched his drink, planted a bony index finger at the base of the shot glass and slid it towards Pymm. "Yer health, mister," he said pointedly.

"Noo," murmured Pymm, cringing visibly. "It smells horribly foul."

"Sufferin' succotash!" cried Old Mundy, his eyes widening alarmingly. "Drink up, youse hear?"

"Noo," murmured Pymm obstinately.

Was it going to be an ugly scene? I wondered, with a sudden sense of panic.

The old prospector's lower lip twitched, his brain apparently churning at a furious pace. Finally, he lowered his grizzled face to Pymm's, and standing eyeball to eyeball with him, planted his gnarled hands squarely on the little man's shoulders.

I tensed, ready to leap into the fray, but Old Mundy remained calm.

"Ah'm gonna try muh level bess tuh talk some sense inter youse, yuh hear?" he said, in measured tones. "So's youse bess listen good."

"I will listen to you, old man," murmured Pymm, "but I will not drink that foul substance."

"Wahl now, we'll jess see 'bout thet," snorted Old Mundy, jabbing a finger into Pymm's chest. "Youse 're a Per'noy'n, ain't youse?"

"Yith."

"En youse worships the truth, don' youse?"

"Truth and *ollagooh*, and perhaps *Goor*."

Old Mundy blinked at that, before continuing.

"En youse cain't deny eny lergical argyment, kin youse now?"

"Noo, logic is one of truth's many tools."

Old Mundy winked at me furtively then leaned towards me.

"Ah learn't thet stuff from them other critters," he whispered, then sniffing menacingly, he turned a baleful eye back on Pymm. "Now this here's muh reas'nin'. Ah 'grees thet the hooch's pure p'ison. Ah 'grees tuh thet, but it's the custom a this here place tuh drink up eny drink offer't a man, eny drink, whatsoorever, en whin a feller don' oblige, wahl, ah jess punches him out." He flailed the air with a knotted fist. "En, ah don' care a hoot if'n yer from outta space 're not. Youse bess guzzle down thet whiskey en be snappy 'bout it."

Pymm immediately bolted down the "foul" substance without a murmur, and as soon as the shot glass hit the bar, Old Mundy had it filled to the brim again.

Numerous whiskies later — having moved to one of the round drinking tables — we were now chatting cozily. Old Mundy was boisterously ranting — punctuated by the occasional reflective sucking of his gums — on how he had first come to be in the desert.

"B'lieve't 'r not gents, ah use'ter sell aut'mobiles out Truckee way. Seems as ah sol't the same Ford tuh two diff'rent gents en had tuh high-tail't outta thir. Jeez! Thet wuz, oh, forty years back now. Bin diggin' fer gol' ever since, ah reckon. Ain't foun' nothing though, nothin' worth a dern. Enyways, nowadays, it's 'ranyum, cupper... stuff like thet."

"Seen any uranium ore around here?" I asked.

"Carn'tite? Shorre. Bin pokin' down this here 'bandon't coal mine. Thir's a bit a carn'tite down thir, but nothin' worth sniffin' at."

Pymm suddenly let out a horrible groan. He had not taken to the whiskey, or it to him, and I certainly sympathized, for my own head wobbled precariously.

I reached out tentatively, gripping his arm, to comfort him. It was as stiff and unyielding as a wooden board!

"You okay?" I muttered.

"I yam erlive, Ne'rman, I th-think," he murmured, "buhht, Oold Mundy, pwease tell us 'bout the l-landing b'foor I pash out."

I flushed with embarrassment. Here I had been gabbing idly away, and had forgotten all about the *First Crossing*, our reason for being in the desert in the first place.

"Lemme see," mused Old Mundy. "Whir wuz ah?" Though his eyes had misted over, he otherwise seemed to be handling the whiskey better than either Pymm or I. "Oh yeah. As ah tole youse, ah brung them critters inter town fer a drink."

"At night?" I asked questioningly.

"Yip, wif thet coyote moon a shinin', en, as ah wuz a sayin', jess showin' dissert hospitoolity. Wahl then, we jess sorta drunk't 'rselves inter a state. Me? Why, ah jess keel't over when the hooch reach't muh chin." He chuckled good-naturedly. "But them Per'noy'ns, Lordy, why they froze't up like a couple a cactuses. Thet's all ah 'members 'fore ah pass't out."

"And when you came to, what happened then?" I asked.

Old Mundy stared cross-eyed into his empty shot glass.

"Truth is, when ah open't muh eyes, why them critters wuz gone. Never saw'd 'em again."

"Did you return to where the spaceship landed?"

"Shore did, in the mornin', but it warn't thir no more."

"And you never saw it or them, again?"

"Never."

Old Mundy's account seemed puzzlingly vague. I tried to remember what Pymm had told me about the *First Crossing's* landing.

As far as I could recall, soon after it landed, Broom explored the vicinity of the spaceship while Elsymm remained inside. A single U.S. plane — probably not a biplane — flew overhead then dis-appeared. Moments later, while Broom was still exploring outside, warplanes attacked the spaceship. Broom, then managed to scurry back inside the First Crossing, *which apparently, had not been damaged, and flew to another location. They returned two days later, and with no warplanes in sight, Broom once again began searching in the vicinity of the spaceship, this time, for what he described as a strange "sand creature."*

Communication was then lost for eight hours. When it resumed, Broom's final transmissions were in broken fragments. First, they indicated that the warplanes had reappeared. A short period of silence followed. Then there were indications that they were being attacked, presumably by the warplanes again, wherein Elsymm had perished and Broom, himself, was mortally wounded.

The final transmission was that Broom had, apparently, despite being wounded, buried the First Crossing *deep under the sand.*

Evidently, during the eight-hour period of lapsed communication, Old Mundy had contacted the Paranoians and had invited them "inter town fer a drink." It seemed odd that afterwards, he had missed most of the action while apparently "pass't out" — not only the attack that had killed Elsymm, and eventually Broom, but the burying of the First Crossing *under the sand, as well.*

"Did you see or hear any warplanes at any time?" I asked.

Old Mundy hesitated as though searching his memory.

"Nuh," he replied finally.

I had the distinct impression that Old Mundy was hiding something. His story was too short, too simple, too unembellished. And how could anyone not hear or see warplanes flying overhead?

"Have you told anyone else your story?" I asked.

"Dern it, this here's a ghos' town," replied Old Mundy. Then he jumped to his feet. "Hol' on a min't."

He dove behind the bar, reappearing a moment later brandishing a crumpled sheet of newspaper, which he proceeded to spread upon the table, ironing out the creases with his forearm.

"It's news when a critter from outta space sets foot 'n Rattler Gulch," he wheezed.

Huddling over his lean coyote body, I glimpsed an account in blurred Gothic print — with atrocious spelling and punctuation — of the landing of the *First Crossing* in the desert. It was too difficult to decipher in my current state so I backed away.

"It's all here," he sniffed proudly.

"Both landings?"

"Yippity, yip."

"Who wrote this?" I challenged.

Old Mundy slapped his knee merrily.

"Shucks! Ah plumb forgot tuh mention it. Ah'm also the ed'ter a the *Gulch Rattle*, cir'lation, one hunnert. Yip! Thir's only one thin' ah ain't 'n this here town — en thet's the unnertaker."

"A hundred," I repeated. "Why so many copies?"

"Fact is, sonny, ah keeps 'em fer the crapper."

At that moment of divine revelation, Pymm uttered a deep groan.

"We musht wift the bluried *slaucer*," he murmured.

"He's a bit whoozy from the whiskey," I explained.

"What's he mumblin' 'bout?" asked Old Mundy.

"The *First Crossing's* buried in the sand, near where the *Second Crossing* landed. It didn't fly off somewhere like you thought."

"Fancy thet," replied Old Mundy, staring at his feet.

"We musht wift it out, we musht wift it out," slurred Pymm.

"How'd it git burie't?" asked Old Mundy.

"It buried itself," I replied dismissively.

An unexpected silence followed, broken only by the sound of Old Mundy smacking his gums, and, from outside the saloon — the lonely moan of the desert wind.

"We'll just have to try and dig it out," I said finally.

"How deep is it burie't?" asked Old Mundy.

"Shoo verry deep," moaned Pymm.

"We'll need shovels," I said turning to the old-timer.

"Shovels?" snorted Old Mundy. "Youse'll need a bullderzer."

"It will w-wift out," murmured Pymm.

"Youse're really gonna try tuh git 'er out?" sneered Old Mundy, his eyes bulging with wonder.

"We are," I said with finality.

"It will w-wift out," repeated Pymm softly.

"Youse're both plumb loco," growled Old Mundy.

"That's possible," I said, with a thin smile, "but we're also determined to rescue that spaceship. You see, old fellow, it's the only way Pymm and his *suum-mate*, Poothy" — the blood surging recklessly through my veins at the thought of her — "can even hope to return to Paranoia. We must do what we can to help them."

"Dern it, dern it," grumbled Old Mundy, shuffling his feet, agitatedly. "Mark muh words, if'n we tries tuh dig up thet saucer, wahl, dern it, thir'll be hell en tarnation tuh pay."

"Why? We're not digging up someone's grave," I said, laughing lightly — immediately realizing that if Broom's body was still on board the *First Crossing*, then that was exactly what we were doing.

As Pymm rose shakily to his feet, I took his arm in support, and together, we tottered towards the entrance to the saloon. We had not gone half a dozen steps, when a low sniveling whine sounded from behind.

My first instinctual reaction was that a dog, or coyote, had somehow slipped unnoticed into the saloon, but I soon realized that the sound had actually issued from Old Mundy himself.

Tears were seeping down his face, and astonishingly enough, his whole twisted frame seemed to be coming unglued.

"Gorsh ah'm sorry, real sorry," he whimpered, his eyes, like two red onions, "jess 'bout everythin' ah guess, but it shore does git lonely 'roun' here. Now ah'm truly glat thet youse fellers show't up, 'specially youse Per'noy'ns. Always know't thet one day thir't be aleens 'n the desert. Never dream't ah'd see it wif'n muh own eyes though."

He sighed long and deeply, the sigh of a very old man. Then, the most astounding thing of all happened next.

Old Mundy slinked up to us like a dog that had misbehaved, and extended a shriveled paw, not to me, but to Pymm.

"Ah wishes youse critters alla the bes'," he sniveled.

"Woo are a twoobled creature," murmured Pymm, accepting the handshake.

Old Mundy rubbed his eyes.

It was a warm and tender moment.

"You'll come with us?" I asked softly.

"Someone's got tuh show youse how tuh dig now, don' they?" he replied, with his coy coyote smile.

Chapter 12 – An Uprooting Endeavor

A SULTRY HALF-MOON HUNG SILENTLY overhead, bathing the ghostly procession of insignificant mortals in a soft, eerie light. Old Mundy — still outfitted in my brown corduroy suit — held the lead, the saloon shotgun cradled in both hands, two belts of shotgun shells crisscrossing his chest in old Mexican outlaw fashion. As for me, surprisingly enough, I had gradually become acclimated to the crazed old prospector's foul garments — the initial itching having mysteriously disappeared.

"Keep yer eye peel't fer rattlers!" he gummed. "The crazy li'l critters jess loves the moonlight."

"I'm sure if they see you coming they'll keep their distance," I said pointedly, dragging a pick and shovel.

Old Mundy had insisted that I carry the main digging implements — he himself being the bearer of the weaponry, which he explained with the old desert adage "Youse never knows what tuh expect 'n the dissert."

Meanwhile, Pymm kept repeating that we had to try and "wift" it out implying that though the *Second Crossing's orgasm* was weak it might still have enough "juice" to do some heavy "wifting."

We skirted the black rocks where Old Mundy said the entrance to his mine was, and some time later, sighted the *Second Crossing* lurking in the sand like a silver crab. Presumably, Poothy was still inside dealing with her "personal reasons."

"If the *First Crossing's* buried under there," I said, indicating the shallow crater, "Why isn't the sand more disrupted?"

"It's the win'," sighed Old Mundy, with uncharacteristic softness. "It blows everythin' smooth like. See, not a speck a veggietation."

And upon closer inspection, I realized that Old Mundy's theory appeared to be true. It was astonishing. Nothing grew in our immediate vicinity, nothing, not the tiniest prickly pear, or cholla cactus, not the spindliest yucca shrub, or sagebrush. Not even the barren desert could be that barren. The process of burying the *First Crossing* had evidently dug up every last living piece of vegetation and churned it into the ground, and then after some days, the wind had smoothed out the sand.

As Pymm tottered up to the *Second Crossing*, a portal mysteriously opened in its side, and he stumbled through it, the portal closing behind him, leaving no sign of its being there.

Old Mundy and I retreated to the safety of a root-bound mesquite hollow about four hundred yards away. There was no need, nor any inclination, for either of us to enter the spaceship.

"What's he need his bury't saucer fer enyways?" grumbled Old Mundy, stamping his feet, impatiently. "Why don' he jess use 'is own?"

"Well, Old Mundy, it seems that there's a malfunction in the..." I started to say.

"A malfooshun?" gummed Old Mundy.

"Yes, a malfooshun," I repeated, "a weakening of the *orgasm*."

"What 'n tarnation's a 'ergasum'?" he growled.

It wasn't that easy a concept to explain to a sun-dried old desert prospector, though ultimately, I slowly began to realize — he might have had more experience with the concept than I.

"It's a kind of engine," I explained, "but it doesn't work properly. Pymm hopes the buried one's in better condition. It's his only chance of getting back to Paranoia."

Our attention was suddenly drawn to the spectacle of the *Second Crossing* rising gracefully above the sand. And as it did so, there was something different in the desert air, something electrifying, a crackling sound, like breaking crystal, emanating from every direction, and increasing steadily in volume, until eventually — it seemed to penetrate my very being, and I found myself clawing savagely at my skin.

I immediately thought of the alien-shield, but it was an entirely different phenomenon. And Old Mundy, too, was affected, hooting and stomping about like a madman. Then the sand itself began to lift, and swirl, and buffet us mercilessly.

"San' storm!" shrieked Old Mundy between yelps.

But I knew differently, and although brutally beset by that extraordinary phenomenon of wind and sand, I witnessed yet another drama unfolding slowly before us.

A gigantic mound of sand had mysteriously risen up onto the desert floor directly beneath the *Second Crossing*. It lingered there motionless for several seconds, then like some deformed prehistoric beast, rose unsteadily to its haunches, crouching for an instant, before springing upwards and settling midair, just beneath the *Second Crossing*, all the while, metamorphosing from prehistoric creature — into the less prepossessing form of an immense sand cone.

With the crystal crackling sound at its peak now, the magically linked spaceship and cone, began slowly moving away across the desert floor — and with the sound beginning to fade, we were soon once again engulfed in the desert stillness.

Neither Old Mundy nor I had spoken, and now, still mesmerized, we watched as, in the distance, the cone disintegrated and plunged earthward. Seconds later, a muffled rumbling echo broke the stillness.

"Thet Per'noy'n's trickier'n a corner't gopher," panted Old Mundy, as we trotted towards the huge crater torn from the sand.

"Paranoians do have a way of creeping up on you," I admitted — an image of Poothy flashing through my mind.

"It's a bloomin' flyin' saucer shovel," declared Old Mundy.

We reached the rim of the crater just as the *Second Crossing* — having returned almost unnoticed — landed softly nearby.

Moments later Pymm joined us. Three heads peered into the depths of the crater. There was no trace of the buried spaceship, just a deep, jagged hole.

"Are you sure it's down there?" I muttered cantankerously.

"Dern it!" jawed Old Mundy. "Cain't we jess leave't alone?"

"We can't," I protested. "If we don't try, Pymm will be trapped on this hideous planet forever."

And as soon as I spoke, I realized that I had used Pymm's word "hideous" to describe Earth. And why? I had no idea. I was a loyal earthling — and kind of liked the "hideous" planet I was living on.

A second maneuver with Pymm's spaceship was deemed necessary. Once again the crystal crackling sound returned — and a second giant cone was drawn from out of the crater, and hauled away. But on this occasion — viewed from our distant vantage point — several small avalanches of sand broke prematurely free from the cone, and plummeted earthward.

The spaceship's *orgasm* was quickly losing its efficacy!

On the third and final trip, all of the sand cone broke loose before the spaceship had scarcely gotten under way, and when the *Second Crossing* came to rest lightly beside the enlarged crater, Pymm emerged from the portal, followed by Poothy.

Peering down into the huge crater in the sand — there was still no sign of the *First Crossing*. It seemed that our venture was doomed.

"It's completely impotent," murmured Pymm dispiritedly.

"So it seems," I replied.

"Poothy and I, we'll never leave this odious planet."

"What a fix, what a fix!" hissed Poothy.

"There is one possible solution," said Pymm, staring at me intently. "With your help, Netherman, we might…"

"Forget it!" I shrieked. "I'll never enter that *saucer*, or any other Paranoian *saucer*, ever again!" Then, beaming maliciously, I added, "but don't despair, Pymm, you might grow to like Earth — eventually."

"Never, never, never," chirped Pymm.

"He'll never grow to like Earth," insisted Poothy indignantly.

"Gittin' down tuh bus'ness," said Old Mundy, pointing to the crater, "thir's still a heap a san' down thir."

Suddenly, Pymm's legs began to wobble, and his face began to twitch.

"Oh no!" I groaned, not another pink fit!

"It won't wift out, it won't wift out," he cried repeatedly.

"We've got to help them!" I shouted, unable to bear Pymm's torment. "We've got a pick and a shovel, let's start digging."

"Youse're plumb loco," wheezed Old Mundy. "Fer one thin', youse jess cain't dig str'ight down, en what would youse do wif'n the fill, eat it?"

"And Pymms, and I can't possibly help," interjected Poothy.

"Why not?" I demanded.

"We detesst sand!" she hissed, with such ferocity that everyone jumped back, including Pymm.

And once again, we were at an impasse.

Pymm was so distraught that his legs buckled under him, and as he sank down into a deep crouch — like some primitive earth-man bending to nature's call — he began to wail in a fit of utter wretchedness.

Old Mundy's eyes bulged with wonder.

"It's a pink fit," I said matter-of-factly. "He's having a pink fit."

"Pymms' *ollagooh* is weak," explained Poothy.

"Soun's jess like cryin' tuh me," grunted Old Mundy.

"Pymms never cries," hissed Poothy venomously.

"Yuh know, ah jess hates cryin'," grumbled Old Mundy, and to my immense chagrin, he, too, seemed on the verge of an emotional breakdown. "Cryin' jess, wahl, it jess tears me up," he continued, wiping his snout in his sleeve, then he, too, began to whimper like a wounded animal.

"What a queer creature!" snipped Poothy.

"Queer is only the beginning," I muttered disconsolately.

Then to my complete and utter consternation, the "queer creature" — his cheeks now swollen pepper-red — sidled over to a mesquite tree, and wrapped his knotted arms around it, as one would a trusted mule.

"Ah jess cain't take't no more," he wailed unabashedly. "Meercy me, alla youse, please stop yer blabberin'. Ah confesses, ah confesses."

"Confess," I grunted. "Confess to what?"

The old coot's jaws were working incessantly now — as though chewing, like breathing, was a prerequisite for life. And whatever it was that was tormenting him, it was something that he was reluctant to reveal.

But finally, the words did seep out, one drip at a time.

"Thir's this tunnel a runnin' unner thet thir crater."

"Tunnel!" I snapped. "What do you mean, tunnel?"

Old Mundy's jaw dropped apologetically.

"Folks, ah confesses thet ah bin diggin' me a tunnel from muh mine t'werds thet bury't flyin' saucer."

"A tunnel!" I barked, kicking a prickly pear in anger. "But you just said we couldn't dig holes, or tunnels, or … and wait, didn't you say that you thought the *First Crossing* had disappeared? How did you know that it was buried here, enough to start digging a tunnel?"

The man was an abject conniving low-down lying scoundrel!

"Ah guess ah fibb't," replied Old Mundy, his eyes mournfully round and contrite. "Wif'n the confooshun en all."

"Well, what did happen?" I demanded.

"Wahl, ah reckon ah daid return in the mornin' like ah said. But ah saw somepin truly made me sick tuh muh stomach."

"The desert wasn't empty, with the spaceship gone?"

"No siree, it warn't," he said, his shoulders sagging.

"Damn it, Old Mundy, what did you see?" I demanded.

"Jeez! It's hard tuh say, 'n front of them Per'noy'n fellers."

"Get it out, you old coot, and the sooner the better," I replied.

"Wahl now," said Old Mundy, wiping his snout in his sleeve. "Thet flyin' saucer was a sittin' thir like a giant silver dollar."

Silver dollar? From what dried-out old well did he get his metaphors from? I wondered — before recognizing that it was probably the same dried-out old well I got mine from. I had this theory that there was a well somewhere in the middle of the galaxy

where everyone drew their metaphors from, and it was drying out
fast. Of course, it wasn't a real theory — just another dried-out
old metaphor.

"An' thir was these arrplanes a buzzin' overhaid," he continued.

"So you did see warplanes. Were they shooting at the spaceship?"

"Yip!" said Old Mundy, after a brief hesitation, "they wuz a shootin' all right."

"And did you see Broom and Elsymm?" I asked. "Were they still outside the spaceship?"

Old Mundy blinked furiously.

"Now thet youse mention it, they wuz," replied Old Mundy, scratching his head, trying to remember a traumatic incident. "One a them was a lyin' 'n the san', still as a stick, while t'other, why he hopp't inter the flyin' saucer."

"And what happened next?" I prodded.

"Wahl then, thir wuz this kinda lull. The arrplanes had gone, en wahl, truth be tol', thet saucer jess dug hisself down inter the san'."

"Dug into the sand?"

"Yip. Then, ah jess skeedaddle't outta thir."

"Where did you go?"

"Ah hid in the mine fer a spell, en when ah ventur't back, wahl thir wuz nothin' thir."

"No sign of a spaceship?"

"Noope. T'was unner the san' ah guess."

"No Paranoian lying stiffly on the sand?"

"Noope."

"No warplanes?"

"Nothin', jess the dissert is all."

"So, Old Mundy, you knew the spaceship was buried here. Why did you start digging a tunnel towards it?"

"Jess curious, ah guess. Thought ah'd jess poke inter't a bit. Ah didn' mean no harm, no siree. Now ah'm shore thet Mr. Pymm here — en the missus, likewise — has need a thet saucer more'n ah do, en thet's why ah's please'tuh offer 'em the full en proper use a muh tunnel, as fer as it goes."

Meanwhile, Pymm had recovered, somewhat, from his pink fit, and standing solidly on his two feet once again — like a penguin, albeit a blue one — extended an arm towards the old prospector.

"You are mowsht kind, Old Mundy," he murmured politely, his tongue evidently lagging behind his body, in recovery.

"You *are* kind, Old Mundy, yet exceedingly weird," hissed Poothy.

And so, quite surprisingly, everything appeared to be settled, at least for the time being. Old Mundy's tunnel — though probably nothing worth "hootin' home" about — was nevertheless our only hope in reaching the *First Crossing*.

Darkness had quietly filtered through the dusk, so it was time to set plans for the night. Pymm offered us the use of the *Second Crossing* for shelter, but Old Mundy proclaimed that he'd rather "kiss a horny sidewinder" than enter any flying saucer.

And on that issue, the old reprobate and I were in perfect harmony.

As it was, we all decided to spend the night out on the open desert.

We built a campfire from tumbleweeds and mesquite driftwood, mainly, to keep away the rattlesnakes. "They jess loves the moonlight," sighed Old Mundy, from time to time — seemingly a mantra of his — as the flames leaped higher and higher. It was quite a memorable sight, those tumbleweeds burning, each a fleeting skeleton of orange — crinkling and crackling into darkness.

Old Mundy curled up into a ball, his head propped comfortably against the stock of his shotgun, while Pymm and Poothy lay directly on the sand, side-by-side upon their backs, arms folded neatly upon their chests.

I lay beside a miniature yucca tree — a perfect six-inch specimen — reminding me of my own dear yucca plant back in Linksville.

We fell asleep with the desert half-moon leering contumeliously down upon us.

Chapter 13 – The Institute

I AWOKE, DRESSED IN A well-tailored gray pin-striped suit, sitting on a wooden bench facing a small amphitheater — a semicircle of outdoor chessboards lying under an overhanging protective roof. It was a park of some sort, one that I was vaguely familiar with.

A moment later, I fully recognized it.

It was Central Park in New York City.

But what was I doing in New York City, and not Nevada, or even Linksville for that matter? I wondered.

At least it wasn't that weird Ataraxia on the planet Paranoia.

But most disconcertingly, it wasn't a dream, and certainly not a nightmare. It was reality!

A quick glance at my hands revealed, reassuringly, normal pinkish skin. I began to relax, somewhat. Everything seemed to be back to normal, or almost normal.

But why, I began to wonder, *were there no other people in the park?*

I rose, and walking along a narrow, pebbled path, came to a lake, again, vaguely familiar, but again, there were no people about, no skyscrapers above the tree line, no cars honking in the distance — which I somehow believed there should be.

I shivered with a newfound uneasiness, and kept walking towards what I believed to be the edge of the park.

Passing under a stone bridge, I saw — in the distance, above the tree line — the soothing white outlines of tall buildings. And once again I relaxed. It *was* the park from the deeper recesses of my mind, one that I was quite familiar with, but then, quite unexpectedly, everything faded.

Consciousness found me in a room, evidently a normal hospital room, with the usual equipment found in such rooms, some of it secured to the wall in back of the bed — and an open window with a cool breeze sweeping in. Its starkness, solidity, and even its excessive brightness, were reassuring.

A man with horn-rimmed glasses, frizzy white hair, and wide laughing eyes glided into the room.

The name on his white doctor's gown read: Dr. Weidelman.

"Good morning, Mr. Steuben," he said, "glad to see that you are with us once again."

"Steuben?" I cried. "You've got me mixed up with someone else. My name is Netherman. And what do you mean by 'again'? And where the hell am I?"

"Ahh," he replied softly. "It must be the trauma. According to Admissions, you are a Lester von Steuben, and, frankly, you have been here with us for quite some time."

"Oh my God! And what trauma is that?"

"Just relax, and don't be alarmed when I tell you, Mr. Steuben," he said, sitting on the edge of the bed, causing me to tilt towards him, "that you were involved in a, shall we say, 'incident'?"

"An incident?"

"Well, it was more of a confrontation, actually."

"Can you be more specific?"

"You were mugged."

"Mugged?"

"Yes, in Central Park."

"Central Park, New York?"

"Yes, in fact, the park isn't far from here. If you look through your window you can just see a bit of the tree line from here."

"And where exactly is 'here'?"

"The Institute, Mr. Steuben."

"What Institute?"

"The Mundy Institute for the Mentally Defective."

"Mundy? M-u-n-d-y? Are you sure?"

"Of course."

"Oh shit!"

"Now, now," replied Dr. Weidelman admonishingly. "We don't permit such language here."

"What type of 'institute' is it?"

"It's a privately owned psychiatric institute, Mr. Steuben. Old Man Mundy — who owns and operates the Institute — changed its name recently from Mundy's Insane Asylum to its present friendlier title."

"And you are a, a…?"

"A shrink? Yes."

"I don't understand."

"That's perfectly normal, Steuben," said Dr. Weidelman, laughing in an unsettling manner. "There's a lot I don't understand, too. Welcome to the club."

"But I'm not mentally defective, Doctor. I merely wake up in different places," I protested.

"Perhaps it feels that way, Mr. Steuben, but look at it from our perspective. You were attacked in Central Park by a gang of thugs, beaten severely on the head with a lead pipe. At one time you had several lumps on your head. Now there is only one — but still a rather sizable one, I'm afraid. You were in a coma for quite some time, and just now, wonderfully, I might say, have pulled out of it."

"I've been in a coma?" I asked disbelievingly, feeling the back of my head — and the monstrous lump lying thereupon.

"Yes, for quite some time, as I said. Occasionally you'd come out of it, but only briefly, before you relapsed once again."

"I don't remember any of it."

"That's not surprising. You were barely intelligible each time that you became conscious."

"What do you mean?"

"You were babbling nonsense," he said, looking at me benignly.

"Would you mind getting up, Doctor?" I asked suddenly. "I keep rolling into you. It's very uncomfortable."

"Oh of course, Mr. Steuben," replied Dr. Weidelman, jumping to his feet. "My wife tells me that I have a terrible bedside manner."

"You have a terrible bedside manner with your wife?"

"No, no, with patients, Mr. Steuben," he replied huffishly.

"About this coma, Doctor, in what way was I unintelligible?"

"Well, for a start, you kept talking about little blue men, and, and — some sort of an invasion."

"Invasion?"

"Yes, from outer space. We actually get that a lot."

"I suppose you do."

"Yes, after a while, you pretty much have heard it all — though in your case, your tale is rather unique."

"Unique? In what way?"

"Your accounts were somewhat consistent, and rather detailed."

"So my 'babblings' were not entirely unintelligible?"

"Yes, Mr. Steuben, in a sense, but I must say that today, you seem remarkably coherent and in good spirits."

"Frankly, Doctor, I feel terrible."

"Oh?"

"For one thing, my head aches."

"Ah. It must be the lump on your head. I'll have the nurse bring you a couple of aspirins. Now, Mr. Steuben, I have other patients to tend to, so you rest. I'll be back later."

And with that he turned to leave.

"But, but, I've so many questions to ask," I protested, "and I've been resting for quite some time now, you know, being in a coma?"

"Right, of course," replied Dr. Weidelman abruptly. "The nurse will be with you shortly. If you have an emergency of any kind, you can always press that big red button."

"You mean the one that looks like the red nose on a clown?"

"There's only one red button there, Mr. Steuben," he sighed.

When the doctor had gone, I tried to reach the red button, but it was just out of reach, and when I stretched out to press it, my head hurt even more, so I eased back onto the bed.

Soon, I was fast asleep, awaking a short time later with a desperate urge to urinate. But I wasn't alone. I was lying naked on my left side, my member extended, a bedpan close by — with a nurse making the necessary adjustments.

"What are you doing?" I cried, immediately taking offense.

"Something I've been doing for months now, Mr. Steuben," the nurse replied casually.

"Well you can stop it right now, Doris," I declared defiantly, reading her name tag.

"Okay then, can you get up by yourself?" she asked solicitously. "You have been immobile for quite some time."

Doris was a middle-aged, stout blonde with an oily freckled face that reminded me of Shelley Winters.

"Let me try," I said, and with some effort, was able to sit up.

Eventually, with some effort, and Doris's assistance, we managed to deposit me in the washroom, where to my great satisfaction I was able to relieve myself, standing up, supported by my left hand pressed against the wall. The words "leech the leprechaun" were scrawled above the urinal — with an arrow, thoughtfully, pointing down.

But the physical effort in "leeching the leprechaun" was *doubly* draining, so I shouted for assistance, but Doris didn't respond, evidently having gone in pursuit of other duties.

Eventually, I managed to straggle back to the bed, enormously pleased with myself. Taking the two aspirins left on my bedside table, along with a sip of water, I immediately lapsed into a deep and peaceful sleep.

I awoke in the middle of the night shivering, a cold breeze wafting in through the open window. My mind, peaceful in sleep, was now in turmoil again. Stretching full length, I reached the red button and pressed it, then waited. Ten minutes passed and no one responded.

Struggling to my feet, I tottered over to peg on the wall where a dressing gown hung, and put it on. Its warmth was comforting. Then, with a surprising surge of strength, I strutted over to the window and looked out, anxious about what I would see.

I immediately relaxed.

It was the bright lights of Manhattan twinkling in the darkness.

But why didn't I wish to see an outline of the streets of Linksville, dismal though it would be? I wondered, as I straddled back to the refuge of my bed. *Maybe it was the sparkle of the Manhattan lights that had attracted me, and I wanted, at least, for the moment, to escape my dreary life, a life that had never been that satisfactory. Truthfully, I couldn't remember much of my Netherman existence — except for the boy from down the hall, and Sukh, the Mongolian on the second floor.*

One persistent, disturbing thought, however, was that the sense of where I was at each lucid waking moment, be it Linksville, Nevada, Manhattan, or even Paranoia, seemed real enough — though always, the sense of who I really was, wasn't. Still, in my core, I rebelled at being considered a "Steuben," and certainly, a "Noothy."

Depressing as it might seem, I wanted to be a "Netherman."

Extremely weary once again, I crawled back into bed and immediately fell asleep. Later, in the morning, I would grapple with the problem of finding out … who I really was.

Doris awakened me at 6:00 a.m. to give me my medication saying that it was for my nerves. I assumed that it was a tranquilizer, but later, when nature called with an unexpected urgency, I realized that it was a laxative. Apparently my bowel movements had become constricted during the coma.

"When did I get here, Doris?" I asked.

"What do you mean?"

"On what date did they bring me here to the Institute?"

"I'm not supposed to tell you personal things, love, but for you, I'll take a quick peek." She raised a pair of round black-rimmed glasses to her eyes giving her an owlish look. "It's barely legible. You know how these doctors have their own scrawl," she continued, glancing at the chart attached to the foot of the bed, "but, it appears that your admission date was December 25, 1977."

"Christmas day?"

"Seems so."

"What day is it now?"

"January 6. It's Epiphany."

"Wonderful, are you Catholic?"

"Yes, and you?"

"I'm not even sure I'm human."

"Come, come, Mr. Steuben," she replied sympathetically. "But I do understand. It must be troubling given your — your condition."

"And what condition is that?" I asked testily.

"You know?" she replied, mildly perplexed.

And then, for the first time, I fully realized that perhaps I did have a "condition"— maybe more than one.

"One thing puzzles me, Doris. I know that Dr. Weidelman said that I've been here for quite some time, and you said that you've been doing that bedpan thing for months, but according to the dates, I've been here less than two weeks?" Doris lowered her head. "What year is it, Doris?" I asked fretfully.

"It's… it's 1979."

"Oh shit!"

"Mr. Steuben!"

"Sorry, Doris, but it's not easy to absorb."

"I understand, Mr. Steuben."

"One other thing, Doris," I continued, "would you humor me and not call me 'Mr. Steuben'?"

She stopped in the midst of puffing up my pillow.

"What should I call you then, love?"

"My real name is Netherman, Lester Netherman. But I hate the name 'Lester,' so you can call me 'Netherman'... or 'love' if you wish."

"Okay, love," she replied, with a ruddy Shelley Winters blush.

"It occurs to me that someone must have bathed me over that period of time, was it...?" I began to say, laying my head back onto the puffed-up pillow.

"Me? Oh no, Mr. Steuben, I mean, love. That would be Oya, the attendant. She does the bathing. It's a skill of its own."

So was helping a man in a coma urinate, I concluded.

"Oya is a woman?" I asked.

"Oh dear, yes. She's from Borneo, a strong but gentle woman."

I sighed deeply.

Despite all the doubts addling my brain, there was one thing I was sure of — and that was that I was a very private person and felt a deep sense of having been invaded.

"One last thing before you go, Doris," I said softly. "Could I speak to Dr. Weidelman? There are so many questions..."

"Certainly, hun, but I do believe that he and the others will be looking in on you momentarily."

"The others?"

"Yes. It seems that several doctors have taken an interest in your case and plan to meet with you sometime this morning."

She started to leave again, then stopped, and removed a bunch of drooping flowers from a vase on a table by the window. Apparently they once were buttercups.

"Who brought the flowers?" I asked.

Someone had evidently taken an interest in me! Who could it be? I wondered hopefully.

"Oh, that was the Flower Lady."

"The Flower Lady?"

"Oh not a lady really, it's Harry Tubbs, one of the patients here. He brings flowers to all the male patients once a week."

"Why did you say 'Flower Lady'?"

"Well, we all think of him as the 'Flower Lady.' Poor Harry once had a relationship with a true flower lady, from the Bowery, I believe. She died from TB and he never recovered. Eventually, he ended up here. I suppose the flowers are his way of remembering her."

"That's a sad story."

"There are a lot of sad stories in the building."

"Stories from the patients?"

"Yes, and from the doctors, too — mainly from the doctors."

"Have I had any real visitors since I've been here?"

Doris put her right index finger against her lips, something she did when she was thinking.

"There was one visitor, but that was quite some time ago," she said finally. "A man in a brown corduroy suit."

"Brown corduroy? What a coincidence! That's my favorite kind of suit. He came here to visit me?"

"Yes, he said he was your agent."

"My agent? What kind of agent?"

"I don't know, love."

"Do you know anything else about him?"

"Sorry, hun, you'll have to speak to Dr. Weidelman about that," she replied before bustling out of the room.

I laid my head back onto the pillow.

God help me, I moaned. *God help me.*

Chapter 14 – The Coal Mine

I AWOKE WITH A RATTLESNAKE sniffing at my boot. An instant later a blast from Old Mundy's shotgun sent the writhing, mortally wounded creature hurtling across the sand.

"Mornin' folks," gummed Old Mundy, "time tuh git goin'."

After much grumbling and whining from the two Paranoians, we collected our equipment — that is Old Mundy and I, the two Paranoians seemingly barely able to support themselves, with Poothy even hinting that perhaps Old Mundy could help carry her — and headed out in the predawn. At the entrance to Old Mundy's coal mine — partially obscured by tall palo verde bushes and hidden among the black rocks — was a mound of weathered wooden planks and rusted ironwork.

"The tipple," gummed Old Mundy, "whir's they use'ter tip the coal carts."

Tucked away just inside the entrance was a small storage area cluttered with a variety of ancient mining equipment:

picks, shovels, crowbars, a wheelbarrow, a wooden coal cart, two battered headlamps, a small quantity of explosive black powder, and an archaic hand drill — all caked in soft dank coal dust.

The accumulation of mining equipment made me wonder why Old Mundy had insisted that I drag a pick and shovel all the way from Rattler Gulch, then I realized that he had done so out of plain orneriness.

"Thir still'n 'missible condition," muttered Old Mundy, donning a headlamp and handing me the other. Out of courtesy he had offered the two headlamps to the Paranoians — but both their heads had disappeared entirely inside the headlamps when they had tested them, rendering them useless.

We loaded the wheelbarrow with the pick and shovel, and with me in front, and Old Mundy wheedling the stubborn jolting wheelbarrow from behind, we started down the sloping mine shaft, our headlamps casting swaths of yellow light before us.

Pymm glided alongside the wheelbarrow, his hand resting lightly against its frame for support, while Poothy crept along in his shadow.

"What keeps the ceiling up?" I shouted, after trudging a distance.

"It's a room en pillar mine," scowled Old Mundy, pointing upwards, "thet's dern hard coal, no need fer support."

Minutes later, we passed a heap of rusted iron.

"Bust't water pump," jawed Old Mundy.

Then, after an eternity of toe-stubbing and stumbling, during which time we passed through a region of intensely pungent air — "meth'n gas," according to the old prospector — past a mass of "dirty carn'tite ore" and a gold-quartz vein "not worth the peckin'," until we finally came upon a small jagged opening chiseled into the end of the main mine shaft.

"'Tention folks!" announced Old Mundy triumphantly. "Ah's proud tuh 'nounce the commenceration a muh tunnel."

"What an odious man, and what odious air!" hissed Poothy, who, in spite of her words — did not seem at all out of place in the cool, stifling atmosphere of the mine.

"The bloomin' fan's bus' but thir's a arshaff down a ways," snorted Old Mundy. He placed a soiled boot atop a small stack of rough-hewn lumber, and peered into the tunnel. "'Bout time the diggin' stert't," he grunted, making no move to enter the tunnel — nor did Pymm who stood gently quivering nearby — nor did Poothy, her head swiveling unnaturally, as she contemptuously eyed her surroundings.

A silence ensued.

"I'm not much of a digger," I mumbled finally.

"One a us needs tuh git stert't. Might as wahl be youse."

"Why don't we both dig?" I protested.

"Ain't 'nough room fer two standin' side by side. So here's what we'll do. Youse'll go firs' wif'n the 'barra. Jess digs the san' en fills the 'barra. Give a holler whin yer ready en ah'll help youse drug't out, thin we'll do a switcheroo."

"Where'll you be while I'm digging?"

"Ah'll be waiting out here whir the arr's fresh."

"Hell!" I retorted.

"Do not squabble, earthlings, please," murmured Pymm, wrapping his arms around his torso. "It's soo cold."

"And what about you, Pymm, old sport?" I snarled, a sudden rage surging through my veins. "A little work would warm you up — and you're the one who wants to leave this hideous planet."

"Oh noo," replied Pymm stubbornly, "I am incontestably unsuited for any sort of labor. Look at my arms, they are soo weak."

He offered me a limb for inspection, and he did have a point. His arms reminded me of celery stalks — without the corrugation.

Confronted with a cantankerous old coot, and the irrefutable persuasion of a man encumbered with celery stalks, I acquiesced, and crouching, entered the jagged tunnel.

"Jess keep yer haid down en youse'll be okay," shouted Old Mundy, with toothless encouragement

Almost immediately, I stopped, and turned to face Old Mundy.

"There's just one thing that bothers me."

"Yeah?" gummed Old Mundy.

"Where's the sand?" I asked, puzzled.

The walls at the start of the tunnel were made of hard coal rock.

"Holy Jeez!" fumed Old Mundy. "Ah already daid the hard part, bustin' through the coal. So, youse jess crawl down the tunnel a ways, en whin youse come tuh the timber overhaid, youse'll be outta the coal bed en inter the san'."

I nodded. But one last concern still remained.

"How do you actually dig the sand? Is there a special technique?"

"Leepin' lizerts!" bawled Old Mundy, his eyes flaring menacingly. "Hack en hew, hack en hew! Jess hack en hew wif'n yer pick, then shovel it inter the barra', youse lunkhaid."

The tunnel was dank and dark and unprepossessing, the only comfort being the dusty shaft of light from my headlamp. Reaching the spot where the coal bed ended and the sand walls began, crude timber supports — each, three segments of wood forming the Greek letter π — were wedged in every six or eight feet. I continued on to the end of the sand tunnel and immediately began dutifully hacking and hewing, hacking and hewing, as Old Mundy had instructed.

Hours passed, sweat-filled suffocating seemingly unending hours, as Old Mundy and I slowly drove a crude twisting tunnel into the bowels of the earth. Fortunately, the sand was firm enough that we decided to risk setting up only the occasional wooden π support. It was a risk, of course, but one we both readily agreed upon.

Conversation was minimal but I did ask Old Mundy one question.

"How do you tell direction down here?"

"Deerection's in muh bones," was his terse reply.

In the midst of it all, on the fringes of delirium, I fantasized about Old Mundy and me as private investigators, a daring team of trouble-shooting desert moles, willing and able to tackle any can of worms — sandworms, of course — as long as they were underground.

Old Mundy was no slacker, laboring at double my pace.

It was I who eventually demanded that we quit for the night, and resume digging in the morning.

Pymm was visibly upset.

"Earthlings," he murmured, wildly waving his celery stalks, "we musht not stop digging, we musht not stop."

Evidently the thought of one more night spent on the planet Earth was too much for him. A mild pink fit was the consequence.

But we did stop digging. For one thing, I was ravenously hungry, and for another, my wretched body pulsed with pain. In particular, my head pounded — with an orchestra of a thousand tiny picks madly hacking and hewing inside my skull.

And Old Mundy, quite understandably, would not continue without me. So finally Pymm was forced to swallow his pink fit, and our gangly band of moles trudged wearily back up the mine shaft, and — no one wanting to spend two consecutive nights on the open desert — along the arroyo to Rattler Gulch, and the hospitality, as it was, of the saloon.

Chapter 15 – At the End of the Tunnel

OLD MUNDY WAS WITHOUT QUESTION a sneaky low-down desert rat.

Leaving the breakfast table the following morning, after naively savoring "steak en frie't aigs" with a slightly exotic flavor — at first attributed to Old Mundy's special seasonings — I discovered *en route* to the coal mine that we had actually feasted on rattlesnake meat and lizard eggs, hairy lizard eggs.

Old Mundy drew one from his pocket for my inspection.

"Thir ain't eny chicks 'n Rattler Gulch, what youse 'spect?" he grumbled by way of apology.

I retched right there in the arroyo much to the wonderment of Pymm and Poothy who had breakfasted on their dubious tiny "food" capsules.

At long last the hours of dreary toil were at an end.

We, that is, Old Mundy and I, had finally broken through to the *First Crossing* and had even cleared away access to a small section of smooth, seamless metal. At the entrance to the coal mine, an immense heap of loose sand lay piled alongside the palo verde bushes.

It was time to collect Pymm and determine whether he could enter the spaceship from where we had reached it, or if more digging would be required. I was exhausted and desperately hoped that the digging had finally ended. Obligingly, Old Mundy offered to crawl back up the tunnel to its entrance and retrieve Pymm, leaving me crouching alone, waiting, in the stifling stillness of the dead end.

The dim fluttering light from the headlamp glanced eerily off the surface of the mysterious metal, inviting me to touch it. Reaching out, I stroked the surface with timorous fingertips, and recoiled.

The surface was hard, and cool, and trembled like a living thing!

My thoughts then shifted to the spaceship's alien-shield, and I shivered.

What if the shield was suddenly turned on, deliberately, or even accidentally? I wondered. *It was easy to panic — stuffed inside a hole, under a mountain of sand.*

Suddenly, I heard soft mouse-like scuffling sounds coming from the tunnel. Moments later Pymm appeared, alone and unsmiling — holding a headlamp in one hand — and a lump gathered in my throat. It was entirely possible that Pymm was only minutes away from leaving Earth, forever!

"Where's Poothy?" I asked, unsure of what to say.

"Waiting at the entrance to the tunnel," murmured Pymm.

"And Old Mundy?"

"Resting with his barbaric weapon. He says he's on the lookout for mine rats."

"Pymm?" I said hesitantly, a number of worrisome thoughts still tormenting me. "We still don't know what really happened to the *First Crossing*. There were only Broom's garbled fragments and Old Mundy really didn't tell us that much. Why would warplanes attack the spaceship in the first place, something must've led up to it?"

"Pure barbarism," murmured Pymm.

"I don't think it was that simple, Pymm," I countered. "Are you sure there weren't any weapons, weapons of any kind, on board the *First Crossing*?"

"None," whispered Pymm.

"But why would they attack an unarmed spaceship?" I persisted. "Did the *First Crossing* attempt to communicate in any way?"

"Was that necessary?" replied Pymm, a wave of irritation rippling across his otherwise implacable features.

"Was that necessary?" I mocked. "An unidentified alien spaceship just can't lurk about, Pymm. If you don't communicate your peaceful intentions, how would you expect the Air Force to know? It's a matter of survival."

"Survival!" quivered Pymm. "Killing is survival?"

"It's kill or be killed when dealing with alien invaders," I retorted, regretting the words almost immediately.

"Barbarians!" hissed Pymm, squeezing past me and letting his lithesome fingers probe the metallic surface of the spaceship.

"What are you doing?" I asked.

"Seeking an invisible portal," he purred.

"Did we get lucky, is there a portal here?"

"There are portals everywhere, Netherman."

"Amazing."

"*Le saucer* is a flexible, almost living thing. Where there is space behind the surface, a portal can be created."

Suddenly, a small black pinprick appeared in the glimmering metal, the opening quickly growing into one broad enough to accommodate the stoutest of earthlings, even Rufus Mulligan.

"Enter, please doo," urged Pymm, pressing a hand lightly against the small of my back.

"I-I don't want to," I stammered.

The gaping portal was decidedly unnerving.

"What doo you fear?"

"Nothing. I have nothing to fear," I lied, firmly resolved to never enter a Paranoian spaceship again.

Pymm eyed me stonily for a few seconds then slipped quietly through the portal and out of sight. The portal remained open, tempting — and terrifying.

Alone once again, I took a deep breath of the cold, stifling air, and soon was even on the verge of relaxing somewhat, when a second small black pinprick appeared on the smooth surface of the spaceship, a few feet to the right of the open portal. It quickly grew into a small circular opening about an inch in diameter, and immediately, an absolutely horrific stench engulfed the small, confined area — the unmistakable odor of rotting flesh!

I scrambled frantically back up the tunnel, banging my head repeatedly against the tunnel roof, arriving at the tunnel entrance, still deep within the coal mine, in a state of claustrophobic frenzy.

Old Mundy, his face twitching erratically under the yellow glare of the headlamp, greeted me.

"Youse smells worse'n a stufft buzzert," he gummed.

I leaned against a smooth coal wall struggling for breath, unable to speak for several minutes, until a series of sinister sounds began emanating from inside the tunnel, strange, scuffling, unfamiliar sounds.

What was it? I wondered, giving in to paranoia. *An image of Pymm hauling Broom's dead body along the passageway suddenly materialized in my mind.*

Old Mundy raised his shotgun ominously.

We waited apprehensively as the scuffling sounds grew louder. Finally, Pymm emerged from the tunnel entrance.

He was alone, and definitely not dragging Broom's dead body with him — or in the company of a squad of little blue men, which I confess, I had also secretly feared.

"What was that awful smell, Pymm?" I asked.

"That," murmured Pymm, his eyes shining with a distant softness, "was the *gratoor*, used for the disintegration of gentle Broom."

"That second small hole in the spaceship was an exhaust pipe?"

"In effect, yes," replied Pymm, before turning towards Poothy, barely discernible in the inky darkness. "Good news, Poothy, my charm, the *First Crossing's orgasm* is functioning perfectly."

"At last," hissed Poothy.

"Thank *Goor* for a healthy *orgasm!*" I sang cheerfully.

Pymm frowned.

"We shall lift the *First Crossing* out of the sand," he said finally, "then land again. We must return to the *Second Crossing* for — for various odds and ends."

I nodded, a swelling in my throat. The leave-taking would not be easy. I had admittedly grown fond of the little blue man from Paranoia.

"Now, hol't on a min't thir!" exclaimed Old Mundy suddenly. "Youse jess cain't hop inter thet flyin' saucer jess yet."

"Why not?" I demanded wearily.

The tiresome old coot was proving to be a nuisance yet again.

"Whin thet saucer busts outta thir," snorted Old Mundy, "the whole bloomin' shaf'll cave 'n — en ah don' aim tuh be bury't live."

The old codger did have a point, I had to admit. Nevertheless, there was a simple solution to the problem.

"Pymm will simply delay the takeoff long enough for you and me to return to the surface," I replied.

"Fiddlesticks!" snapped Old Mundy mulishly. "They's a comin' wif us tuh the top en thet's thet!"

"That's absurd!" I cried, disgusted with the old man's stubbornness. "Why, they'd have to hike up the mine shaft, then turn around, and hike all the way back down again, and for what, for nothing. That's preposterous!"

"Mebbee so," snarled Old Mundy, baring his gums, "but thet's what thir' gonna do."

I was about to protest yet again, when Pymm gripped my arm.

"We shall doo as Old Mundy says," he murmured. "Old Mundy knoows about sand."

I had no reply to that, and being increasingly aware each passing moment of the capricious and eccentric nature of the cast of characters surrounding me, let the matter stand.

Once more, we started up the mine shaft.

On the way up, however, I had another sudden dizzy spell — *and my mind slowly drifted into unconsciousness.*

Chapter 16 – Not Quite Hysteria, But Close

WHEN THE DIZZINESS IN MY head had faded, I found myself back in the Institute. Doris, I recalled, had just left the room. Moments later, alarming scraping, scratching sounds emanated from the hallway. I immediately imagined a herd of approaching rats. But soon, Dr. Weidelman scuffled into the room followed by two doctors, all in white coats.

Dr. Weidelman greeted me cheerfully.

"How are we doing today, Mr. Steuben, have a good sleep?"

"No," I replied testily.

"Nothing like your own bed, is there?"

"Probably," I muttered, "if I knew where my *own* bed was."

"In time, with patience, we shall all endeavor to find out where that may be," replied Dr. Weidelman, glancing knowingly at the other two doctors, both smiling thinly. "My associates are present here merely to observe, at least initially."

Dr. Lekarz Zloty, according to his name tag, reminded me of a chemist, or even an undertaker, despite the white gown. The other, a small short bushy mustachioed man with slough eyes, had his name tag upside down. With some effort, I made out the name Dr. Shim — thinking that while pinning his name tag to his gown, Dr. Shim had made sure that his name was clearly visible — to himself.

"You are looking surprisingly good," continued Dr. Weidelman.

"Oh, do I?" I replied with a hint of sarcasm. "Well, I do *not* feel good, and I am baffled, to say the least. And please stop addressing me as 'Mr. Steuben.' I am Lester Netherman, and I'm not from New York. I'm from Linksville, B.C."

"And where do you think you are now, Lester? May I call you that?"

"No! I don't like the name Lester, either. It reminds me of … oh, never mind."

"Then what should I call you?"

"Netherman would be acceptable," I replied, deciding that "love" would not be suitable in the case of Dr. Weidelman.

"Okay then, Netherman. May I repeat my question then? Where do you believe you are right now?"

"It seems to be New York City. Manhattan, in fact."

"Good, good, good. And how do you think you got here?"

"Now that is a really good question, Dr. Weidelman," I replied.

"Yes it is, and what do you think the answer is?"

"The answer is that I really have no idea."

"Well then, if I may, let me present you with a few indisputable facts. First, you are clearly a Mr. Lester Steuben, and it is an undeniable certainty that for almost two years now, you've been here in this Institute. The entire Institute will attest to that. So, therefore, if there is to be any progress in your case, we must first accept the fact that you are indeed a 'Mr. Steuben.' Do you understand me, Steuben?"

"Doctor, I do admit that this place does seem real, very real. Still, would you mind if I pinched you to see if *you* are real?"

Dr. Weidelman laughed lightly.

"Why not pinch yourself first to see if you're real, or not?"

"I've already done that multiple times, Dr. Weidelman, and it seems that I myself am real, but as for you ...?"

"I understand, Mr. Steuben," replied Dr. Weidelman soothingly. "Such a request, remarkably, is not entirely uncommon. In fact, lately, there's been something of a run on pinching requests among my patients." He offered me his forearm for inspection, a hairy forearm revealing several red marks.

I gently pinched it.

It seemed real enough.

Oddly enough, I immediately got the impression that Dr. Weidelman was himself relieved by my determination that he was indeed real. Perhaps we all need reassurances from time to time.

"Would you care to inspect my colleagues?" he asked mischievously. Both colleagues cringed visibly.

"No, no," I quickly replied.

There was something clinically sinister in their manner, especially Dr. Zloty. Yet, for some reason, I did not have the same sense

regarding Dr. Weidelman. In fact, in him, I detected a sympa-
thetic soul and, for the first time, began to wonder what his issues
were — implicitly assuming that all psychiatrists had problems.
And facing three of them now meant that I had to contend with
three sets of mental disorders foisted upon me all at once — in
addition to my own.

"Are we having a full session now?" I asked suddenly.

"Yes, if you wish. Would you like that?"

"Yes, Doctor. I think I need it."

"Well then, why don't we start and see how it goes?"

"Fine," I replied.

At that moment Doris arrived with a tray bearing a brown paper bag and a bottle of Coca-Cola. Shoving Dr. Weidelman aside, she placed the tray on the bed beside me.

"Here, hun. My treat," she warbled before slipping out of the room.

I opened the bag. Inside it was a foot-long hot dog, Coney Island style. Ignoring the doctors, I savagely tore into the hapless offering like a leopard tearing into an antelope, smearing mustard and splashing diced onions, as well as some of the savory meat sauce, over my hospital gown — not that I intended to attribute the smearing to any leopard, a metaphor only went so far — whilst the troika of doctors gaped at me with clinical intent.

"I see you have an appetite, that's good," said Dr. Weidelman finally, when the orgy had ended.

"Sorry for eating in front of you, Doc. I was famished."

"Not surprising, Steuben, you've been fed intravenously for almost two years now."

"And what type of diet was that, Doc, not pureed hot dogs, I hope?"

"No of course not, Mr. Steuben. We use a crystalloid solution, Hartmann's in fact."

"Sorry, Doc, just kidding," I replied, wiping the feral debris from my mouth with a towel.

Both of Dr. Weidelman's associates were showing signs of irritation and were apparently on the verge of something sinister. What precisely, I had no idea, though — in a moment of wild speculation — I imagined them opening their white gowns and spraying me with bullets from hidden machine guns.

But that, of course, was an idle psychotic fantasy — and not quite the curse I was tainted with.

"Where would you like to begin?" asked Dr. Weidelman.

"Begin what?" I replied, sipping the Coca-Cola.

"Our session, Mr. Steuben."

"Oh that! How about telling me what you know about me?"

"Well, that seems like a good place to start. When you were transferred here from the hospital, after your head wound was treated, among your possessions was a New York state driver's license in the name of Lester von Steuben."

"I have a driver's license?"

"Yes, you do."

"Where is it?"

"It's in your locker," he replied, indicating a gray locker just to the left of the door, "along with your other possessions, including the clothes you were wearing when the, ah… incident occurred. Would you like to see them?"

"Yes, I would."

Dr. Zloty, deciding to make himself useful — apart from being an "observer" — sprung to his feet and opened the two French doors to the locker. Visible inside was a white pinstripe shirt and a pair of brown corduroy slacks. Ignoring them, he took two items resting on the top shelf, a worn brown calfskin wallet, and a gold-plated Mickey Mouse watch, too shiny to be expensive, and handed them to me with a condescending grin.

I fondled the watch momentarily — idly thinking of the Polish taxi-driver back in Linksville, wondering if he had even existed — then tossed it onto the bed with a "not my style" detachment.

The wallet was far more interesting.

In it was a sawbuck and a fiver, an unused ticket to a Yankees' baseball game — played several months ago against the Boston Red Sox — a brittle stick of chewing gum, a picture of a man who was vaguely familiar and the driver's license.

"Who won?" I asked.

"Damn if I know," replied Dr. Weidelman, looking enquiringly at his two colleagues. Both shook their heads. No baseball fans there.

And as Netherman, I had had zero interest in baseball, or any other sport for that matter — though I vaguely remembered having bowled once.

I inspected the driver's license.

It was issued to a Lester von Steuben, born May 5, 1935, with an address listed as 115 Bleecker Street, New York City.

The picture on the license might easily have been that of a younger me.

"I'm an American according to this?" I said with a frown.

"Apparently, yes."

"Damn. I'd rather be a Canadian."

"You look like an American, especially with mustard and onion bits on your gown," replied Dr. Weidelman with a smirk.

"And this place on Bleecker Street is where I-I lived ... live?" I mumbled, ignoring the mess on my gown.

"Lived," replied Dr. Weidelman. "You were evicted months ago."

"What kind of a place was it?"

"It was a room above a delicatessen."

"Was I evicted for failing to pay the rent?" I asked jokingly, reaching down for a strip of onion on my gown.

"You joke, Mr. Steuben, but there was quite a wrangle over that," replied Dr. Weidelman. "But in the end the Institute settled the matter."

"How did they settle it?" I asked, sucking on the onion.

"We explained that you were in no condition to pay any back rent — fifty dollars, it was — nor was anyone else going to. The landlord was a persistent Greek, but in the end, he gave up."

There was a momentary lapse in the conversation.

I idly examined the photograph of the vaguely familiar man.

On the back of it was the name Sukh.

I shivered.

What was a picture of Sukh, the Mongolian, doing in Steuben's wallet? I wondered, utterly bewildered.

"Ahem," said Dr. Weidelman, clearing his throat. "Do you have any more questions or concerns?"

"Yes, in fact, I have quite a few," I replied, quickly recovering from the shock of seeing the Mongolian's image. "Do I have any possessions from my Bleecker Street residence?"

"Ah yes, you do, Mr. Steuben. We were given a suitcase packed by the landlord, hastily, I might add."

"And where is the suitcase now?"

"It's in a special storage area in the basement of the Institute, a place for larger personal items belonging to patients."

"May I see it?"

"Of course, I'll have Doris look into it."

"Thank you, Doctor, now, can you tell me anything else about me, what I did for a living, did I have any friends? You know, what kind of a guy was I?"

"Indeed, Mr. Steuben, but we actually found out very little. We really don't know what kind of a guy you were, or are, for that matter. We, of course, are not investigators. Dr. Zloty made all the inquiries."

"What did Dr. Shim do?" I asked pointedly.

"Well, he-he..." stammered Dr. Weidelman.

"I'm strictly an observer," interjected Dr. Shim defensively.

"You said that I was first taken to a hospital after the incident," I pressed on. "What hospital was it?"

"Yes, it was St. Agnes'."

"Is St. Agnes' a big hospital?"

"No, in fact, it's very small, but it was the closest hospital, and you were in serious condition."

"I see. Didn't anyone at the hospital check into my identity?"

"Not the hospital specifically, but I do believe that the police did go to your residence. They found the Greek uncommunicative, and left. Nothing further was done, until we got involved."

"How long was I in St. Agnes'?"

"A couple of weeks or so."

"And you said that Dr. Zloty made the inquiries?"

"Yes, I did. He likes collecting information. Perhaps, you can take over, Doctor," said Dr. Weidelman turning to his colleague.

"By all means, glad to do so," said Dr. Zloty, approaching the bed. "Let me begin, Steuben, by saying that I find your case exceptionally intriguing and promise to remain at your side until all is resolved."

"You don't mean that literally, I hope?" I said.

"Actually, I do," replied Dr. Zloty seriously. "Getting back to your landlord, does the name George Zakarias ring a bell?"

"No. He's the landlord?"

"Yes, well, we told him about the incident, and that you were in a coma, and he immediately began wrangling over your back rent."

"He didn't show concern for my condition?"

"Not that I noticed. Do you remember anything at all about him, what he looked like, and perhaps your relationship with him?"

"No nothing, Doctor, I told you, I don't remember anything about my life in New York, if indeed, I had one."

"The evidence on that issue is clear, Steuben, and as Dr. Weidelman has suggested, the sooner we accept that, the better. Now, Mr. Zakarias did eventually say something interesting, however."

"Oh?"

"Yes, that you had an agent, the man who visited you some time ago, a man in a brown corduroy suit."

"Oh yes, Doris mentioned him."

"Apparently, Steuben, you are a writer?"

"Ah yes. I do recall, in my 'other life,' having written a modest novel or two," I replied, thinking of *The Earth Eaters*.

"It wasn't that sort of writer."

"Oh, what kind was it?"

"Apparently, you were a technical writer."

"Heavens, what's that?"

"Someone who produces owner's manuals and user guides for various types of equipment. Your agent said that you were particularly talented with writing stuff for appliances that 'blew air.'"

"God help me! What does that mean?"

"He was referring to hair dryers and vacuum cleaners, I believe. He said that you had basically 'sucked up' the entire New York market."

"What an awful metaphor!" I cried soulfully. "So Mr. Zakarias pointed you to my agent?"

"Yes. You apparently had given Zakarias your agent's name and address as a reference."

"What is my agent's name, by the way?"

"His name is Morty Achers. His office — if you can call it that — is essentially a telephone service for a handful of clients, nothing more than a tiny room in a lane off of East 23rd Street — with a single wooden desk, receptionist, a telephone, and a two-drawer filing cabinet. Your name was on a board on the wall, you know, one of those things with replaceable letters."

"You went to see him and told him what happened?"

"I did."

"And then he came here to the Institute to visit me?"

"Yes. I received him. Dr. Weidelman was off on an emergency of some sort. Doris was also here, of course."

"How did he react when he saw me?"

"He seemed sad."

"He didn't leave me anything, like flowers, or …?"

"No, but he did leave me his telephone number. Do you want it?"

"No thanks, Doc. I believe my technical writing days are over. Did he happen to mention a wife, or perhaps a girlfriend?"

"Sorry, Steuben. He said he knew nothing about your personal life."

"Oh shit!" I moaned, suddenly overwhelmed with despair. "What kind of a man am I?"

"Here, here, Steuben. It's not so bad. These things take time."

"Yeah, but what about St. Agnes'? Did I have visitors there?"

"We were told that there were two."

"Indeed, and who were they?" I asked, brightening up —
not that I believed a word about being this "Steuben" character.

"Well, a priest came to see you for a week then
stopped coming."

"Maybe he discovered that I was an atheist."

"I think he thought that you were no longer near death."

"And who was the second visitor?"

"An older man who said that you might be his long-lost son,
and when he saw you, he immediately attested that you were."

"He said I was his son?"

"Yes, but it soon became obvious that he was a fraud,
that he was attempting to gain some advantage from being
your father."

"What tipped you off?"

"He was dressed like a bum and smelled awful."

"Still, he might have been telling the truth?" I
replied defensively

The idea of having a tramp for a father rather appealed to me.

"No, not that it transpired," continued Dr. Zloty. "When
he kept insisting on seeing your possessions, we became suspicious and contacted the police. We discovered that he was in
the habit of visiting local hospitals claiming to be the relative
of people, either in comas, or with acute memory loss. It was
a scam."

"Doc," I said, yawning suddenly, and feeling very sleepy, I
drifted off into unconsciousness, wherein I had a somewhat
unsettling dream of being a guinea pig — a mentally defective
one — in a strange lab.

I slept most of the afternoon, in spite of the chilliness of the room, and when I awoke, Doris was by my bedside mooning me. Not "mooning" in the crude sense, but adoringly, watching me while seated in a chair.

How long had she been there? I wondered.

Evidently, it had been for a prolonged period, for she had a small portable table by her side on which were three empty Styrofoam cups, some donut crumbs, the leftover crusts from a sandwich, and an ashtray filled with ashes and cigarette butts — though she was not presently smoking a cigarette. There was a faint trace of smoke in the air, however, despite the window being wide open with a cold evening breeze sweeping in.

"How are you feeling, hun?" she said.

"Drowsy," I muttered.

"Dr. Weidelman spoke to me. We've stopped the medication. It's all part of your recovery process."

"Thanks. Were you sitting there long?"

"Oh no, not at all," she replied huffily. "I was just on my break, had to take it somewhere."

"I'm famished," I said.

"I'll run and get you a Coney if you want," she said eagerly.

"Would you? That would be nice, two of them, maybe?" I replied. "Did you pay for the last one out of your own pocket?"

"Oh no, love. It was my treat, but I used a ten from your wallet. It wouldn't be proper to pay for a patient's meals. Someone might think... oh you know what someone might think."

I didn't know what someone would think. How could I, I barely knew what I thought?

Still, I nodded knowingly.

"Is Dr. Weidelman still around?" I asked.

"No, but Dr. Zloty is. I saw him in the Doctor's Smoking Room with Dr. Shim."

"Were they talking about me do you think?"

"Oh no, love, they were just sitting there smoking."

"They were smoking without speaking to each other?"

"Yes. I hope I'm not talking out of school, but they seem to have trouble talking to people, in general."

"Frankly, Doris, I find them both rather creepy."

"Well, Dr. Zloty is actually the chief psychiatrist in the Institute, and he *has* taken a special interest in you, though Dr. Weidelman is officially in charge of your case."

"I like Dr. Weidelman a bit more. What do you know about Dr. Shim?"

"Dr. Shim? He's an odd duck. I'm not really sure what his connection is with the Institute. He just seems to loiter about the place. Never says anything that sounds like a doctor, and I would know, of course, I've been here for more than twenty years. No Freudian references, no medical jargon, just casual conversational stuff, but only in response, never initiated."

"Maybe he's an alien?"

Doris laughed gaily.

"I agree with you, hun, he does look creepy. But, Dr. Zloty does seem to approve of him."

"You know what I'd like to do?" I said suddenly.

"What's that?"

"I'd like to pinch both of them to see if they're real."

Doris jumped to her feet, a sudden look of concern on her face.

"I'll get you those Conies, love, and a Coke."

When Doris had left the room, I laid my head back on the puffy pillow and stared aimlessly out the open window.

Hope came and went, fleetingly, it seemed. At the moment, it had fleeted.

Chapter 17 – Paranoia, Encore

A COLD BREEZE RUSHED IN through the open window, causing a swath of white curtains to billow — like the tattered sails of a ghost ship.

Curtains? I wondered. *There were no curtains in my simple antiseptic room in the Institute.*

Slowly, I adjusted to my surroundings.

I was lying in a bed in what seemed to be a stone hut, with a curtained window and an open doorway, and clearly not my room in the Institute, or even that amorphous room in — oh where was it now — Ataraxia?

So where was I, Earth, Paranoia — or somewhere else?

I suppressed a scream.

Though seemingly skeptical in my attitude towards Dr. Zloty, I had grown rather comfortable with being Steuben. Then I noticed that I was wearing a strange close-fitting robe — of the kind worn by Pymm!

"Ah, you're awake finally," murmured a familiar voice.

And there in the open doorway stood Pymm.

"Hello, Noothy," he said, approaching the bed. "Don't try to rise. You've just recovered from a terrible nightmare."

"A nightmare," I replied, "but where am I, Pymm?"

"You're on Paranoia, of course," he murmured. "You've always been on Paranoia."

"But everything's so different. Where is that strange room, the one without walls and floors, and ...?"

"Ataraxia? You were moved here to the Stone Oasis. We thought it would be less disturbing after your most recent relapse."

"I had a relapse?"

"Yith, Noothy."

"Damn it, Pymm. My name isn't Noothy. It's ..."

I wasn't sure how to reply. I wanted to be Netherman, but then again, maybe I was this Lester Steuben. I had to admit, Dr. Zloty had been rather convincing.

"Okay, Pymm," I continued. "But please, call me Netherman, or even Steuben if you wish. Both names are acceptable, for the moment."

"Steuben? That is new to me, but sure, I'll try to remember that," he replied, unconsciously rolling his eyes. "Now, as I was saying, you've had another relapse. Do you remember when we talked last? I had to leave you abruptly?"

"Yes, Pymm. Despite my 'relapses' as you call them, I seem to remember certain things rather well."

"Yith, Noo … Netherman, quite remarkably, you do. And when I returned, you were unconscious and apparently in the middle of a prolonged nightmare."

"It wasn't a nightmare," I moaned. "I was merely somewhere else."

"Ah well, in any case. We immediately moved you here where the environment is less clinical. Sadly, your nightmare, or whatever it was, persisted and only ended a few minutes ago."

"Oh shit!"

"Why not tell me about it?" murmured Pymm agreeably.

And with that, I recounted my experiences on Earth, first in Linksville, then the Nevada desert, and finally, the Institute in New York City — mentioning the doctors, and Doris, and describing the increasingly convincing belief that I was Lester Steuben.

Pymm didn't interrupt me once.

In fact, the recounting took so long that he eventually began nodding his head drowsily.

Instinctively, I trusted him more than I had Dr. Zloty, or Dr. Weidelman, or even Doris, though the most vivid memory of all was of the Coney hot dog I had eaten. In fact, I was hoping that Doris would soon return with the two more Coneys that she had gone out for — though that seemed rather unlikely at the moment.

"Are *you* real, Pymm?" I asked when I had finished my story.

"I've been wondering the same thing about you," replied Pymm, somewhat startled by the question.

We both laughed.

"What interests me," continued Pymm, "is that you seem to be caught up between two narratives, both taking place on this strange planet you call 'Earth,' one in which you say, I, and perhaps Poothy, visited you, and the other involving a place you refer to as 'the Institute,' also on planet Earth."

"But surely, Pymm, you must remember your visit to Earth? You even brought back some Earth specimens with you."

"Sorry, Noothy... oops, Netherman, but neither Poothy nor I have ever left the planet Paranoia, nor do we even have the means to do so. And from your description of Earth, it appears to be far more advanced than Paranoia. I must confess that those were two truly fascinating tales."

"They were not tales," I chided. "Both actually happened."

"So you say," replied Pymm. "Now, you said that you shared a *sensuum* with Poothy?"

"Yes, on the way from Linksville to Nevada."

"Do you realize that that might be disturbing to me, personally — for you to even fantasize such a thing?"

"Oh," I replied.

What else could I say? Was Pymm jealous? Were he and Poothy entangled in some way? Was I, inadvertently, caught up in the middle of some weird Paranoian love-triangle?

"We'll let that go for the moment," continued Pymm. "Now, you seem to be caught between two conflicting narratives, one in which you were Lester Netherman, and the other, Lester Steuben, both from planet Earth. Is that about it?"

"Yes, Pymm, and in addition to that, you seem to think I'm someone called Noothy from the planet Paranoia. So, from *my* point of view, there are three conflicting narratives."

"It's a problem, admittedly. You can't be all three."

"Oh can't I?" I spouted, just to be obstinate.

"Maybe you can believe that you are three different people, but you can't be on two different planets, that is definitely not possible."

"You do have a point there," I conceded.

"And we're both at this moment undeniably on Paranoia."

"So it seems."

"Perhaps we're moving too fast," said Pymm, with a sigh of exasperation, "nevertheless, you did say that Steuben had a head injury. Check your head, it looks fine to me."

I quickly inspected my head.

There were no bandages there and certainly no lump!

"So, Pymm, please, am I really on Paranoia?" I asked pleadingly.

"Yith, most definitely."

"How did I get here?"

Pymm gave me a deep soulful stare.

"You never..." he began.

"Never what?"

"You never left."

I stared back at him disbelievingly.

"But, but that's impossible."

"Look at your arm, Noothy," he said with renewed determination. "What do you see?"

And for the first time I noticed my hands. They had a very faint, but distinctly Carolina-blue tint!

"What does this mean?" I cried.

"The obvious, Noothy, that you're a Paranoian."

"That's absurd! It can't be!"

"Sorry, Noothy, but yith, you were attacked by ..."

"Mungo Beings?" I cried.

"Good *Goor* no!" replied an exasperated Pymm. "There are no such things as Mungo Beings. They were just part of your fantasies."

"What about my novel, *The Earth Eaters*?"

"Come now, Noothy, if there's no 'Earth'?"

"But everything was so vivid, so detailed. I could touch the sand, feel the heat of the desert — and even smell Old Mundy. I even wore his stinky clothes, for *Goor*'s sake!"

"There, Noothy, you just referred to *Goor*, the Divine One, instead of using the word 'God' as you did in your narratives."

"Oh God, my earthly God," I lamented, more to myself than to Pymm. "I never believed in you, but now?" Then I turned to the Paranoian. "You said I was attacked, by what?"

"Well, it was a rather odd attack. You ate too many *ham* berries and it made you drowsy. Apparently you are allergic to them, though they are generally very nutritious. Then while you were disoriented, a *burgee* sat on you, almost suffocating you. My belief is that the oxygen deprivation combined with the allergic effect caused you to hallucinate."

"Why that's preposterous. Everything was so vivid, so vivid."

"Our brains have that ability, Noothy. We all dream, even healthy Paranoians, in a seemingly real way."

"So how then can we tell if we're dreaming?"

"It's a good question," replied Pymm. "I myself might be dreaming. Unfortunately, none of us can really tell for sure. We can only believe."

"Pinching won't help?"

"No, Noothy, unfortunately, it's beyond pinching."

I lowered my head. My heart had been beating madly throughout our exchange, and I needed a moment's rest.

"Are you really a doctor, Pymm?" I said eventually.

"Yith, Noothy, I am, but so is Poothy, and she has been assigned to care for you. She's away tending to another patient at the moment but she'll be back momentarily."

"Damn!"

"Well then," replied Pymm, "for your general health and well-being, I think it's time you started mixing with other Paranoians."

I immediately shuddered at the prospect. Still, despite my recalcitrant behavior, I was beginning to slowly accept the idea of being Noothy — much as I had earlier grown into acceptance of being Steuben. It seemed that I was desperate to settle into any consistent persona.

Then my hand casually entered a deep pocket of my robe.

My fingers gripped a leathery object.

I withdrew my hand.

In it was the wallet from New York with my driver's license in it — and my familiar Netherman-Steuben image!

I stared at Pymm in abject terror.

Chapter 18 – High Noon in Nevada

I TRIED OPENING MY EYES but a harsh sunlight forced them shut.

Where was I now? I wondered.

Finally, the oppressive heat stirred my memory.

I was back on Earth!

All four of us — Old Mundy and I, and the two Paranoians — were back at the entrance to the coal mine.

It was high noon in the Nevada desert — a time when only the bravest most cold-blooded of desert creatures dared stir.

Pymm, his ribbed chest beating irregularly, slouched wearily atop a flat rock, while Poothy, her tall silky form weaving from side to side, towered over him. Nearby, a guileless ground squirrel — surrounded by a protective ring of spiny cholla cacti — nibbled quietly on a dried cactus fig.

"We shall rest then return to the *First Crossing,*" panted Pymm.

I felt a sudden sadness. He and Poothy would soon be returning to the spaceship, buried deep under the sand, at the end of Old Mundy's mine shaft. From there they would "wift" out of the sand, before making the ultimate journey back to Paranoia.

"Will it lift out okay?" I asked, crouching beside him. "There must be tons of sand above it."

Pymm took a slow, labored breath.

"Yith. Mass does not matter."

Old Mundy, fidgeting like an infested jackrabbit, suddenly quit the shelter of the palo verde and took a crouching position near the ruins of the tipple, his shotgun, disconcertingly, squeezed between chest and knees.

"Netherman," quivered Pymm, "during Broom's final set of garbled communications, he first said that they were being attacked. I assumed that he meant by warplanes again, but *now* I seem to recall two later fragments that were single words 'earthling' and 'attacked.' Could Broom have been referring to …?"

He paused mid-sentence, staring fixedly at Old Mundy then at me.

The implication of Pymm's words proved too much of an exorcism for my scorched brain. However, the effort proved unnecessary, for a clear metallic click sounded in that lingering moment of desert dormancy. Shielding my eyes from the sun's glare, I turned in the direction of the sound, towards the black silhouette arched against the horizon, towards Old Mundy fondling the shotgun — now leveled directly at us.

I staggered to my feet.

"Wh-what're you doing?" I grunted disbelievingly.

"Wahl, ah jess guess ah'll hunt me some rattlers now," replied Old Mundy, his voice low and ominous.

"How odd!" hissed Poothy. "He wants to hunt rattlers!"

A huge coal boulder squatted ten feet away.

"Quick, quick," I urged, "hide behind the boulder."

I had suspected it for some time, but I was certain now — Old Mundy was undeniably insane!

"Why?" hissed Poothy imperiously.

"Why?" I cried incredulously. "Don't you see? He's going to..."

"Hunt rattlers," sniffed Poothy.

"Yith, rattlesnakes," murmured Pymm languidly.

"You fools!" I cried, staring at the two naive Paranoians in disbelief. "Don't you see, *we're* the rattlers he means?"

The two Paranoians immediately stiffened.

With a loud curse, I grabbed Poothy's arm.

She slipped from my grasp, spilling onto the sand, an expression of horror marring her features.

"Barbarian!" she spat.

"Queer uns, ain't they?" chortled Old Mundy gleefully. "En what purty faces, too, shore does hate tuh mess 'em up."

"What's come over you?" I shouted, in a desperate effort to delay the demented old-timer.

"Don' make a move," warned Old Mundy, brandishing the shotgun menacingly. "Ah doesn't much take tuh youse, sonny, but ah doesn't aim tuh kill youse neither. Jess step 'side so's ah kin git muh sights on them blue critters."

Pymm, having finally assessed the situation, darted for cover.

I lunged for the unmoving Poothy, and catching hold of her razor-boned ankle, dragged her writhing, mutinous body towards the boulder.

The dreaded roar of the shotgun did not materialize.

"Sssavage!" hissed Poothy, spitting out mouthfuls of sand.

"Hiss all you want, my sweet," I said, once we had reached the temporary safety of the boulder, "but that's a shotgun he's holding."

Poking my head above the jet-black mantle of rock, I spotted Old Mundy poised beside the tipple, shotgun pressed to his shoulder in ready position, but making no move to approach.

I dropped down beside Pymm.

"Can't you do some of that *quarkking* stuff?" I pleaded.

"Noo, Netherman," he replied, his eyelids fluttering anxiously. "It won't work. Old Mundy's mind is too turbulent."

I groaned.

What a predicament! Something had to be done, and quickly. As soon as Old Mundy decided to approach us, our chances of becoming buzzard meat would be buzzard high — if that made any sense.

"Hey, old-timer!" I shouted, leaning out over the curving lip of the coal boulder and squinting against the sun. "How's about you and me going into town for a couple of drinks? My throat's awfully parched."

"M-mebbee later," came the hesitant reply, "but feerst, ah'm gonna plug them aleens full a holes."

Perspiration stung my dry drawn skin, setting my eyes ablaze. I was chained to that damned rock, chained by circumstance, chained by the naked sun. I had to bully myself into thinking, into engaging Old Mundy in conversation — even if only to keep him from approaching the rock.

"Why, old fellow," I called out, feigning friendliness. "I thought you liked Pymm. Hey! You were even drinking with him?"

Low, rasping laughter drifted back across the baking sand.

"Ah always gives a rattler a drink 'fore ah plugs 'im," he replied. "'Tis dissert ettyquette."

"Always? Wh-what do you mean?" I stammered, a sickening sensation in the pit of my stomach.

Never was the desert more still than at that foreboding moment.

"Thet's what ah done tuh them other critters," came the chilling response.

My limbs went limp. I slithered helplessly down the jagged side of the boulder onto the sand, lying in a heap for a minute or so, stunned by the old man's words. It was true then, my deepest fear.

Old Mundy had been the "sand creature" — and had been responsible for the massacre of Broom and Elsymm!

"What-what others critters?" I uttered hoarsely.

I had to know more! Old Mundy was hopping up and down, agitated, yet in a talkative frame of mind.

"Them *Per'noy'ns*, a course. Whin ah whint back tuh thet flyin' saucer wif 'em, why, ah, wahl, ah plugg't 'em both." He cleared his throat in a sudden bout of wheezing and hawking.

"One a the critters scramble't back inter the saucer. Ah 'spect he wuz hurt bad. Ah left th'other fer the buzzerts en high-tail't it outta thir."

Both Paranoians must have heard every word of Old Mundy's confession, for they cuddled up to me like frightened puppies — Poothy's limp form shivering sinuously, Pymm sitting upright, stick-like.

"Welcome to Earth," I muttered.

Suddenly, a thunderclap rent the still desert air, and a wave of pellets splattered the boulder above our heads.

I peered out, tentatively, in time to see Old Mundy re-aim the shotgun — and ducked.

The gun roared a second time.

"Come'n out so's ah kin plug youse," shrieked the crazed old prospector. "Youse're worse'n a commie pertectin' them critters."

Then Poothy's elongated head popped up, high above the rock mantle, swaying like a crane's, curiosity evidently getting the better of her.

I hauled her down unceremoniously.

"Isn't it time we left thiss barren place?" she hissed, her face, once again, pasted with sand.

A Gila monster suddenly appeared from beneath a clump of sagebrush — and with its tongue flicking in and out — crept across no man's land, slipping quietly under a creosote bush.

For a moment it caught everyone's attention.

"Ah kin wait, ah kin wait," muttered Old Mundy, barely audible.

What a hellish predicament, I thought to myself, slumping down between the two Paranoians. *And why didn't Old Mundy just walk over to where we were hiding and shoot us?*

"Come closer so we can talk!" I shouted out impulsively.

Perhaps it was foolish of me, encouraging him to approach us, but I had to find out what was stopping him.

"Naw!" he called back. "Ah ain't goin' near them tricky critters. Ah'll jess stay here en wait for 'em to come out."

With Poothy seemingly having no contact with reality, and Pymm — gallant Pymm — pressed against the boulder like a patch of lichen, I gazed upward in exasperation, at the soft azure sky, streaked with piffling wisps of cloud — and I began to wonder.

How could we escape? Wait for Old Mundy to run out of ammunition? No. One glimpse of the broad belts of shotgun shells garishly crisscrossing his chest snuffed out that notion. Make a wild dash for the entrance to the coal mine? Definitely not. I could not imagine Pymm and Poothy sprinting anywhere.

Finally, an idea did surface, an idea with minimum risk, and therefore, certainly worth trying.

"Hey, Old Mundy!" I called out lustily. "You crafty desert fox. How'd you find out about it?"

"'bout what?"

"You know damn well," I replied, forcing a laugh, "in fact I believe that's why you killed those Paranoians."

"Jumpin' Jehoshaphat! What'n tarnation youse jabb'rin 'bout?"

"Hah! Pymm told me all about it."

"'Bout what, dern it?"

"You know," I teased. "There are tons of it."

"Tons a what, fer Christ's sake?"

"Why, the gold," I said, bravely stepping out from behind the boulder, "all that gold."

"Gol'?" breathed Old Mundy, his knees buckling under him, the snout of the shotgun nose-diving into the sand.

"Yes, gold," I repeated calmly, "on board the buried spaceship."

The stratagem seemed to be working!

The word had a positively hypnotic effect on the old prospector.

My pulse quickened.

"Real gol'?" sighed Old Mundy, his eyes bulging insanely.

"Why yes, but gold bars, not nuggets," I replied. "Maybe you're not interested in gold bars?"

"Gol's gol'," muttered Old Mundy philosophically.

"Now, why don't you put down your..." I began, taking a deep breath, but before I could finish — Old Mundy was slinking across the sand towards us.

"Ah'm gonna plug 'em, thin take a look see," he panted.

"But how're you going to get into the spaceship if you shoot them?" I said, hurriedly, blocking his way.

"Ah'll blass muh way through. Now git outta muh way," he snorted, motioning me aside with the shotgun.

"With that hare-popper?" I laughed. "Warplanes couldn't penetrate that spaceship. How do you think you'll do? No, face it, Old Mundy, you're going to have to talk to Pymm — and be nice about it, too. Come'n now, he's not such a bad sort. Think of all that gold."

"Mebbee youse're right," growled Old Mundy. Then steering me aside with the tip of the shotgun, he peeped behind the boulder. "Youse li'l critters kin come out now," he said, ever so sweetly.

"You are soo oleaginous!" hissed Poothy rising to her feet shakily.

"This here's muh deal, li'l critter," snorted Old Mundy, ignoring Poothy, and poking the barrel of the shotgun into Pymm's stomach. "Youse'll git me some a thet gold en ah'll let youse en yer missus be off'n yer saucer. What d'youse say tuh thet?"

"There is no gold," murmured Pymm.

I was dumbstruck.

How naive could any alien creature be?

"Pymm wants the gold for himself," I quickly interjected, trying to salvage what I could.

"But there is no gold," repeated Pymm.

Poothy — who appeared to be more earth-wise than Pymm — kicked him savagely in the rear, causing him to stumble forward, a shocked look on his face.

The mass of furrows in Old Mundy's brow twitched erratically, as he pondered the situation.

Meanwhile, I was seriously deliberating whether to make a lunge for the shotgun, when Old Mundy suddenly took a step back.

"Git movin'!" he snarled, savagely transformed once again. "All a youse. En be snappy 'bout it! He cocked the shotgun. "We's goin' back down the mine."

There was an air of harsh finality in his voice.

Some time later, we once again stood deep inside the coal mine facing the jagged entrance to the tunnel leading to the *First Crossing*.

Old Mundy was briskly businesslike as he handed Poothy a headlamp.

"On yer haid, missy," he gummed. "En hol't it up wif yer hands so's youse kin see. Now, inter the tunnel, en min' yer step." Obediently, Poothy slithered into the tunnel. "Ah'll jess fooler en …"

"Hold on a minute!" I yelled. "Pymm should go with you, not Poothy. He's the only one who can open the portal to the spaceship."

My reasoning was that Pymm would have a better chance of coping with Old Mundy than Poothy — or so I thought.

"Is thet the truth, Per'noy'n?" growled Old Mundy.

"Noo," murmured Pymm, avoiding my baleful glare.

"Wahl now, we bess be goin', en ah doesn't want youse fellers crawlin' 'n after us, unnerstan'?" grunted Old Mundy, easing into the tunnel after Poothy — his headlamp askew atop his head. Moments later the old prospector's faint voice could be heard from deep within the tunnel. "Foorwoord march now missy, hop tuh't, hop tuh't."

Left behind in perfect darkness, neither Pymm nor I spoke for several minutes. Finally, it was Pymm who broke the silence, his voice rich and confident again.

"Poothy has an insatiable appetite," he murmured peacefully.

I laughed softly, recognizing the significance of his words.

Our troubles were over, at least for the moment.

But why would Poothy share the sensuum with a withered old crock like Old Mundy? I wondered. *Was I jealous?*

On the other hand, maybe there were even stranger matches back in Paranoia.

Chapter 19 – Farewell

AN HOUR HAD ELAPSED SINCE Pymm and I had parted company inside the coal mine. He had crept back down through the tunnel to the *First Crossing*, assuring me that Poothy would easily subdue Old Mundy and be await-ing his arrival. Pymm also promised that the "wifting" would not disturb the timbered mine shafts of the coal mine, and that the *First Crossing* would not immediately depart Earth but would land beside the *Second Crossing* so that we could have a proper leave-taking.

And he had been true to his word.

After groping my way back up the mine shaft to the surface, through unrelenting darkness, I found the two spaceships squatting side by side, gleaming phosphorescently in the waning light of day.

Almost immediately Pymm and Poothy emerged from the *First Crossing*, Poothy sliding effortlessly across the sand towards the *Second Crossing* — where an open portal awaited her — and Pymm trundling over to where I awaited him, sitting upon a driftwood log.

I sensed that the leave-taking would be as heart-wrenching for Pymm as it would be for me. I would miss the little Paranoian. In a little over a week, he had quivered and murmured his way into my heart as no earthling ever had.

"That was rather tidy," I said in greeting. "I expected a massive upheaval of sand. I heard nothing and felt no tremors in the ground."

"Extracting a buried *saucer* with a fully functioning *orgasm* is a simple matter," explained Pymm. "Besides, much of the sand above it was already removed."

I shivered involuntarily at Pymm's mention of an "orgasm."

"How is Old Mundy? Did he survive the lifting?"

"He did, Netherman. He's on board the *First Crossing* resting. He will make a fine earthling specimen."

I laughed.

"So, you finally have your specimen?"

"Yith, the uncouth creature joins the others."

"The others," I cried. "There are more?"

"Yith, Netherman."

"When did you, uh … acquire them?"

"Some time ago," replied Pymm evasively.

And as he finished speaking a portal opened in the side of the *Second Crossing* and a line of earthlings emerged, led by Poothy — her head bobbing back and forth like a woodpecker's.

"Those are your specimens?" I cried out. "They were in the *Second Crossing* all this time?"

"Yith," murmured Pymm.

"But I didn't see any earthlings when we made the jump here?"

"You were, shall we say, preoccupied — for which Poothy and I offer you our eternal gratitude."

The earthling specimens were now moving slowly across the sand — silhouetted against the red eye of the setting sun — towards the *First Crossing* where an open portal awaited them.

"They remind me of the line of dead souls in *The Seventh Seal*," I mused. "Are you familiar with the Bergman movie, Pymm?"

"Yith, Netherman, but I prefer *Duck Soup*," he replied.

The line had almost reached the *First Crossing*.

Five unknown persons of various shapes and sizes, followed by two stragglers, trudged through the sand behind Poothy. The second to last straggler was Rufus Mulligan, but it was the last straggler that captured my full attention.

It appeared to be Sukh, the Mongolian who lived on the second floor directly above me!

"Not Sukh," I blurted out. "You can't take him."

"But why, Netherman? He wants to leave."

"That can't be. He seemed so happy here."

"How could you know that, Netherman? When I asked him about you, he said that he barely knew you, that you and he had never met. Moreover, he said that he finds Earth — particularly, North America — most inhospitable."

"But he's from Mongolia," I protested.

"Yith, Netherman, I know. In fact, he kept asking me, almost wistfully, if Paranoia was anything like Mongolia."

"You've *quarkked* them all!" I screeched.

"Noo, Netherman. We didn't have to. Poothy and I were quite surprised at how many of you earthlings actually want to leave your foul planet."

"But I thought that you liked Earth," I protested. "You seemed curious enough about it, exploring it in your spaceship, before the, err ... the malfunction?"

"Yith, for a time I was curious, but now I am in complete agreement with Poothy. It really is a revolting orb."

"Orb?" I cried. "Now it's an orb?"

"Yith, Netherman, and before I depart, I must repeat my warning to you. You did not take me seriously the first time."

"What warning?" I asked, apprehensively.

Could he possibly be referring to those nasty Mungo Beings again? Hadn't we finished with that nonsense?

"I'm tired of your warnings, Pymm," I continued, in anguish. "We earthlings are always warning each other about something. If it isn't nuclear war, or hydrocarbons depleting the ozone layer, or overpopulation — it's Coca-Cola, white bread, and fudge. No more warnings please, Pymm, no more warnings."

"But I must, Netherman," persisted Pymm earnestly. "Yith, you are aware of many dangers to your planet's survival but you ignore the deadliest threat of all, the invasion from within."

"Come, come, Pymm," I chided, "you sound paranoid again."

"And you are smug, Netherman," he admonished, his granite gray eyes boring into me. "Frankly, I'm disappointed in you. We are trying to help you in your struggle against the Mungoliens — oh, I'm sorry, the Mungo Beings — and then, of course, there's that novel you wrote."

Oh no, not The Earth Eaters *again, haunting me forever! Not on Pymm's day of departure. He had mentioned the novel during our first meeting, believing that it was written as a serious warning, when all it was, was a fanciful work of science fiction, that was, truthfully, both ridiculous in premise, and in execution. And now Pymm was repeating the utter nonsense that the premise was actually grounded in a genuine threat.*

"Goodness gracious, Pymm," I continued, "there are no such things as 'Earth Eaters.' It was simply a shoddy work of fiction."

"Yith, I know that now," murmured Pymm, "and I agree that it was shoddy fiction, and that there are no such things as 'Earth Eaters,' and even as a metaphor, it, well frankly, it stunk — but there definitely are Mungo Beings infesting your planet."

"You've gone bananas!" I cried.

Pymm stared at me, inquisitively, as though I had gone bananas. And he was probably closer to the truth than I was.

"You must listen, Netherman," he quivered. "As I told you before, they are intelligent beings cleverly hiding among colonies of earth viruses and they are determined to destroy all earthlings."

"You are absolutely nuts," I cried, searching his features for some clumsy attempt at humor — but his features were as grim as always.

"We don't have much time, Netherman," he murmured, "so listen carefully. Not every earthling is infected by these Mungo Beings, but you, my friend, unfortunately are."

"You *are* serious!" I replied, in shock.

"Yith," murmured Pymm gripping my hand with his tiny vice-like fingers. "Isolation is the key tactic to use to combat them. They thrive on a complex communication network. Isolation breaks down their communication links, and soo, we Paranoians have developed special Mungo Suits."

Mungo Beings? Mungo Suits? Poor, poor Pymm. The strain of a week on Earth was clearly crippling his judgment.

"Are these Mungo Suits designed only for Paranoians, or can earthlings …?" I began amusedly.

"Oh they fit earthlings, too — if stretched a little."

"How do they work?"

"As I said, isolation is the key. The Mungo Suits not only offer protection from the Mungo Beings, but if the little devils are trapped within one of our special suits, they can't communicate with those outside the suit, and will quickly die."

"And so will the unfortunate soul in the suit, I presume?"

"Unfortunately, yith."

"You touched my hand a moment ago," I said, smiling gently. "Aren't you afraid one of those little Mungo devils will hop onto you?"

"Oh, noo, Netherman. Poothy and I wear special clothing that has the Mungo protective quality customized into it."

"I see, so you're saying that we must make several billion Mungo Suits to protect the earth's population."

"That would be impossible to do," murmured Pymm.

"If you show us how to make them we could set up automated assembly lines, and …"

"Automation won't work. They have to be hand-stitched."

"Hand-stitched?" I asked, dumbfounded.

"Yith, and frankly, it's not something we can teach earthlings."

"Oh my!"

"But, *mon plus cher ami*, Poothy and I have patched together two extra suits. We can leave them with you."

"Two suits! That won't help much, if what you say is true?"

"Yith, I knoow. But you could use one of the suits, and the other you could give to a friend, or a relative."

It didn't seem like a promising prospect for the future of Earth. Besides, I tried to remember if I even had a relative, my mind being such a continuous blur. I certainly didn't have any friends.

"So the planet is doomed?"

"That's what I've been trying to tell you, Netherman!"

"Shit!"

"Still, you could always come with us to Paranoia?"

"No thanks," I snapped.

At that moment of proclamation of approaching doom, a huge form emerged from out of the impending darkness, moving ponderously towards us like a giant tortoise.

It was Rufus Mulligan.

He stopped before us, hands on knees, struggling to regain his breath.

"Hee, hee," he chortled eventually. "I was about to board the other spaceship when I decided that I had to say good-bye to poor old Netherman — not that we ever had any kind of a relationship. Still, you're the last earthling I'll ever see. I suppose I'm a sentimental sap. By the way, what happened to you? Frankly Netherman, you smell awful, and you're covered in — what is that — coal dust?"

"What? Oh that," I muttered — realizing that I was still wearing Old Mundy's foul garments. "I helped Pymm get to the *First Crossing*. It was buried under the sand."

I had no intention of telling Rufus Mulligan the truth.

"How does that explain the coal dust?"

"Oh, I suppose it doesn't," I groaned.

"The *First Crossing*? Is that the spaceship we're leaving on?"

"Yes."

"It's all pretty confusing. I had no idea, and still don't, as to what's really going on, except that it's all good riddance to Earth."

A man freely taking leave of the sanctuary of Earth was, in my opinion — a man freely taking leave of his senses.

"But why *are* you leaving? Don't you realize that to Pymm, you're nothing but a specimen?"

"I'm aware of that, Netherman," he replied, lowering his head with uncharacteristic shyness, "but Pymm advises me that my condition might be curable on Paranoia."

"And you believe him?"

"I don't believe, or disbelieve, but I do dream sometimes. By the way, we'll be traveling with some kind of 'sand creature,' according to Poothy. That should be interesting."

"It's not a real sand creature, Rufus," I laughed. "Poothy has her own distorted view of Earth — and everything on it."

"Well, what is it then?"

"*It* is an old prospector by the name of Old Mundy, and admittedly, he is a creature of sorts, a demented one. He murdered the crew of the *First Crossing*, and tried to murder Pymm and Poothy, too — and me, too, for that matter."

"He murdered an entire crew?"

"Well, there were only two of them. Paranoians seem to like to travel in pairs. And as for Old Mundy, you'll have ample opportunity to get acquainted with *him*. He'll be going to Paranoia with you."

"But what about you, Netherman? Did Pymm invite you to join us?"

"Yes, he did, but there's no way I'm leaving."

"Hee, hee!" laughed Rufus Mulligan. "I'll wager a pound of flesh to a small oyster *hors d'oeuvres* that you'll be aboard the *First Crossing* when she skips off into space."

"Never, never!" I replied animatedly. "Besides, Pymm has all the specimens he needs."

"The only reason you're not roosting in the spaceship right now," roared Rufus Mulligan merrily, "is that, seemingly, for the time being at least, you can't be *quarkked*. Yes, I know all about *quarkking*. Some of us have clearly been *quarkked* but not me. I'm leaving voluntarily. Pymm is cunning, and patient, and I'm warning you, my dear devout earthling — he's not finished with you yet."

"What rubbish!" I growled.

"I'm off!" cried Rufus Mulligan suddenly, and with that, he turned around and began trundling back towards the *First Crossing*.

During my conversation with Rufus Mulligan, Pymm had been standing silently nearby listening attentively, while around us, the desert flatland had surreptitiously darkened into night.

I stole a glance at Pymm watching *Monsieur Avoirdupois* squeeze through the portal into the *First Crossing*.

Pymm's features were as inscrutable as ever, but it would not be in his appearance that I would detect the treachery, if indeed there was any, but in the texture of his voice.

He turned to me, eyeing me sphinx-like, with the early crescent moon leering over us. I shivered, hardly noticing the softly spoken words.

"Come, come on board," he murmured, "only for a moment. Poothy wishes to bid you farewell."

"Why doesn't she come out here?" I muttered testily.

"Poothy will never step foot on Earth again."

"And I, Pymm, will never step inside a *saucer* again," I replied, giving it the usual saucy French pronunciation.

"As you wish," he purred.

"So, all your specimens are nicely tucked away, eh?" I said acidly.

"We *are* ready to leave," he murmured.

"And that oddball Rufus Mulligan is among them," I said with a nervous laugh. "He accused you of trying to trick me, trying to lure me back to Paranoia with you."

"Oh noo, Netherman, noo," replied Pymm, his head jerking back unexpectedly. "We have an understanding."

"That's what I told him!" I declared, with a relieved smile.

And I immediately felt ashamed of myself for doubting the little mulberry blue Paranoian. He had always been forthright and open with me, even to the point of warning me about the Mungo Beings, although that was, undoubtedly, a bit of lunacy. Slowly, anger began welling up inside of me, anger directed towards the fat man.

He could have very well ruined Pymm's leave-taking.

"I must say that Poothy and I will miss you," murmured Pymm.

And there, in an instant, that whipping-cream feeling of intimacy was back again, as thick and unctuous as ever. Tears clouded my vision. Pymm touched my hand delicately, his skin magnetically vibrant — as on the day we first met.

"It seems like you've been here an eternity," I whispered.

"It does, doesn't it?" sighed Pymm, looking up at me, his eyes seemingly rounder and fuller than usual. "Earth is not suited to you, Netherman, it is much too *dur*."

"*Dur?*" I repeated, momentarily confused.

"Harsh, Netherman. Sorry for the French."

"That's okay, Pymm. It's something I'll always remember you by."

"You *should* come with us, Netherman," he murmured, with renewed enthusiasm. "Soon, there will only be a few scattered earthlings remaining, some of them infected, some hiding in isolation from the others. There will be nothing for you here, nothing … nothing."

"Nothing," I heard myself repeating, as my resolve to remain on Earth began to waver.

The wavering quickly gained momentum, like a desert flash flood, until finally — I found myself being propelled irresistibly in the direction of the *First Crossing*.

It wasn't a trance. I was sure of that, nor was my brain clouded or benumbed. All my faculties functioned with their customary clarity and nimbleness, yet, for some inexplicable reason, I was unquestionably moving towards the spaceship.

"Nothing, nothing," I whispered to no one in particular, tears streaming down both cheeks, as a tumbleweed crumbled underfoot.

"Nothing," a disembodied voice murmured from behind

I sailed on giddily chanting, "Nothing — nothing — nothing."

Then suddenly, a dozen paces ahead of me, a host of tumbleweeds leapt high into the air — stirred by a sudden gust of wind. With both arms flailing wildly, I waded through them.

For the most part they were nothing but a nuisance, but then to my utter stupefaction, one of them, bigger and more belligerent than the others, struck my cheek, savagely, tearing my flesh, causing me to stumble.

Almost immediately, a wave of revulsion engulfed me, a revulsion directed towards Pymm, and Poothy, and all things Paranoian — a wave quickly transforming into an urge to flee, to flee away from the *First Crossing*.

I gave in to that urge, and fled as hard and as fast as I could, while from far behind me — as though from a distant world — I could hear Pymm's tremulous voice.

"Come… Nether… man, man… Nether… man, man."

I dared not look back.

After sprinting what seemed like a desert marathon, I stopped to regain my breath, and peering back with some trepidation, I saw the two spaceships gleaming in the distance — giant fireflies in a sliver of moonlight — poised side by side, until suddenly, soundlessly, both of them vanished into the night.

I turned and ran… and ran… and ran.

Chapter 20 – Aftermath

"WHISKEY, WHISKEY," I MUTTERED TO myself as I stumbled into the Rattler Gulch saloon, consumed by one concern, and that was a need for a stiff drink. A bottle of Tennessee Bourbon lay tucked behind the bar — jammed between a soiled Gideon's Bible and a box of shotgun shells. Wrenching off the cap with blistered fingers, I filled a shot glass.

"Ahhrr!" I yowled, as the vitriolic liquid seared my parched throat.

But self-inflicted torture was exactly what I needed, so I poured out a second portion and bolted it down. Sinking into a saloon chair, and gazing numbly about the room, I wondered, not for the first time, just how in hell was I going to get out of that damned desert!

Soon, deep hunger pains sent me reeling into the kitchen in quest of something to eat, but all I could find were thin strips of rattlesnake meat drying from a rafter, and nesting inside a Navajo clay pot, a half-dozen lizard eggs. Hesitating for a moment, I came to the stark conclusion that what had tasted good once would certainly taste good a second time — and commenced stuffing the cast-iron stove with wood.

A meal worth chronicling! I thought to myself sometime later, as I sat lounging in the middle of the saloon, diligently picking at tooth and gum with a thorn thistle.

On the table before me lay a flattened copy of the *Gulch Rattle*. From time to time, in random bits and pieces, I read and reread Old Mundy's account of "The Massacre of the *First Crossing*," how he had single-handedly repelled "a blue invershun a erth using only wits, dissert lore en a varmint gun."

I groaned.

Why had I not read the article more carefully the first time? I wondered. *Old Mundy had, naively, presented it to me on Pymm's and my first visit to Rattler Gulch. It was a complete confession of the brutal murder of Broom and Elsymm — though in the demented view of Old Mundy, it was a glorious heroic escapade.*

But I really couldn't concentrate, my mind drifting eerily in and out of the events of the past week or so. It had seemed so real, yet always lurking in the deeper dark recesses of my mind — and there were many such deep dark recesses — was the unsettling thought that perhaps it had all been some bizarre dream. The bourbon was oddly comforting, though I did miss my special tea and my Bulgarian teacups.

Moments later, I was sound asleep with my head resting on the table.

I awoke the following morning with the sun's early morning rays poking through the open doorway.

I felt wretched.

From just outside the saloon came the unmistakable sound of an engine revving then sputtering to a stop. I remained immobile in my chair, incurious, uncaring, and listless.

A minute later two men burst into the saloon, one, rake-thin and squirrelly, the other — wielding a movie camera — ponderously bearlike.

"Hi, pal," chimed the squirrel. "Name's Munk, side-kick's Biff. We're from KOMA TV, Reno. Say, where in hell is everyone?"

I tried moving my lips, to reply with something intelligible, but couldn't. My brain simply didn't work. I groaned.

"Look, pal," said Munk, his keen eyes skimming the interior of the saloon, "give us a break, will yah? Might even be a few bucks in it for yah. Just tell us where the action is."

"Action? You're nuts, this here's a ghost town," I finally croaked. "Lillie's come and gone."

"He's a stinking loony," snorted Biff, resting his camera on a table. "He won't know fart all."

"This is Rattler Gulch, ain't it?" asked Munk, ignoring his comrade, as he eased into the chair beside me. I muttered something to the effect that it was. "See, Biff, what'd I tell yah? This is that ghost town the whole damn country's buzzing about."

"What's that?" I grunted, with a new sense of alarm.

"Why, according to reports, this is the place where those little blue men from outer space first landed on Earth," he replied.

I exploded into loud, raucous laughter — though I was anything but amused — with a gnawing ache in the pit of my stomach at the memory of anything to do with aliens or alien spaceships.

But Munk, the squirrel, pressed on.

"Face it, bud, it won't be long before the place's crawling."

"It's crawling now," I moaned, and the truth was that everything in the room seemed squirmy and out of focus. "Tell me what you know first, then, well, we'll see," I offered.

"Sure thing, pal," grinned Munk, quickly launching into his story. "Several days ago, two backpackers hiking in the nearby desert sighted some strange blue-skinned creatures. They were human-like, but definitely alien beings"

"The backpackers?" I queried.

"Jesus!" snapped Biff.

"No," said Munk softly, "the backpackers were normal people, but the creatures they spotted were definitely alien."

"Oh!" I replied.

"Yeah, and they were standing beside what looked like a flying saucer, and get this — they were communicating with an earth-man."

"No kidding?" I replied.

"Yeah, that's right. I estimate that the sightings occurred about eight miles west of Rattler Gulch. Now, normally I'd be pretty skeptical, but consider this. Item one: The hikers were highly respected men, a district court judge and a state senator, not men who'd jeopardize their careers on some phony tale. Oh, a little graft now and then, perhaps, but never, never a hoax. There's nothing in it for them, you see? Item two: A similar sighting was reported near Vancouver, Canada, about a week ago, but there's not much known there. You know how reticent those Canadians are? Item three: And this is the clincher. The president — the President of the United States, that is — is flying down to Reno today to take a look around, and if POTUS is coming here to Nevada, well, draw your own conclusions." He gave me a hard expectant look. "It's your turn, pal."

I rubbed my eyes drowsily. Munk's terse delivery had been pure torture. All I wanted was to be left alone, allowed to sink into the floorboards and become one with them.

Nevertheless, I forced my lips to part.

"I-I'm a little under the weather," I mumbled. "Drive me somewhere, somewhere where I can get a pot of tea, and maybe a jelly donut? Then I'll tell you what I know."

"Come on, pal, be serious," whined Munk. "The nearest coffee shop's fifty miles from here."

I do not know what would have happened next, if the rattle-snake had not appeared, but it did, and Biff was the first to hear it.

"Hey, Munk, is there a strap loose under the table, some-thing hanging from the camera?" he asked, searching blindly beneath the table with his left hand. "I hear a rattling."

I was the first to see it, tightly coiled at the base of the bar, a few feet from the table, serene and lethal.

"Look, look!" I whispered, "Against the bar, against the bar!"
The two men stared at me, bewildered.
"The bar, the bar!" I repeated hoarsely.
Two heads turned in unison.
We bolted from the saloon as one.

The drive across the desert flatland through harsh early morning sunlight proved uneventful. After forty or so miles of open sand, we came upon a paved two-lane highway and, a few minutes later, a bus depot café combination. Over a piping hot pot of tea and a jelly donut, I started my tale — a weird concoction of little blue men and spaceships, liberally sprinkled with minutiae from the plot of *The Earth Eaters*. Needless to say, it was a fabrication, and it was not long before my two journalistic friends recognized it as such and stormed out of the depot in disgust.

I prowled the living room of my Linksville apartment zealously tending to my potted plants having neglected them for so long. A week had passed since my return from the Nevada desert, and there had not been a word from Pymm. I had half expected him to rap on my apartment door once more, though logically, I was convinced that he had gone forever.

Still, in an odd sort of way, I felt that he would always be with me.

As far as television, radio, and the newspapers were concerned, the Paranoian crossings might never have been. And apart from an occasional longing, that suited me fine. I was doing well, except for the odd headache and momentary black-out — which I supposed was quite normal after the stress of an extraterrestrial encounter.

Moreover, for several nights now, I had heard the old re-assuring thumping sound coming from the apartment above me late at night, again only for a brief minute or so.

Had Sukh returned, or even left? I wondered. *Had I been mistaken about seeing him boarding the* First Crossing *in the Nevada desert?*

Still, I was comforted that certain aspects of my life, however small, had reverted back to their normal routine — or seemingly so.

There was a faint rap on the door.

My heart pounded wildly as I fumbled with the safety chain.

Could it be Pymm returning for something he had forgotten, or maybe he had changed his mind about leaving Earth — or maybe, just maybe, the orgasm *on the* First Crossing *had developed a malfunction?*

Trembling with anticipation, I opened the door.

"Say, mithter, got eny *oig kertins?*" chirped the boy from down the hall.

Choking on the automatic "no" that had lodged in my throat, I scoured the boy's greasy face.

"Come in," I muttered. "I'll take a look around."

He followed me into the kitchen. There were two soiled egg cartons in the garbage can. I handed them to the boy.

"Gee, thanks, mithter."

I stared at his frail form for an uneasy moment or two.

"Would you like a glass of milk and a jelly donut?" I finally astonished myself by saying.

"Shur-rre," grinned the boy, seating himself at the kitchen table without being told. I poured out a tall glass of cold milk.

"By the way," I said, feeling awkward, "what do you use the *oig kertins* for?"

"Wull," replied the boy, preparing his answer by hunching his shoulders, "my friend, Freddy an' me, we're constrictin' a spaceship."

"Well, well, don't 'constrict' it too much, or it might not take off," I offered teasingly.

"No, mithter, we won't," he replied seriously.

"And when you're finished building your spaceship, what then?"

"We'll fly away."

"Away from Earth, you mean, to a place like Mars?"

"Mebbee further."

"As far away as, as Paranoia?" I asked, with a touch of remorse.

"Mebbee," replied the boy, downing the milk in a single gulp.

"Take me with you," I said jokingly.

"Shure, mithter," he replied, stuffing a donut into his mouth, and another into a pocket. "Gotta go. Thir's a lot more doors ter knock on."

"Come by anytime. I'll save my egg cartons for you," I smiled.

"Gee that's swell, mithter," said the boy, pausing in the hallway, just outside the door — before sneezing mightily.

"You've a cold?" I said sympathetically.

"Yith," said the boy, wiping his nose in the sleeve of his shirt. "My mom says it's goin' 'round."

"It's those Mungo Beings," I replied matter-of-factly.

It had just slipped out!

I closed the door behind him — and immediately upon entering the living room, felt woozy.

Chapter 21 – Dr. Zloty

WHEN THE WOOZINESS FADED, I found myself back in the Institute with Dr. Zloty walking into the room, beaming, as though he had just won the Preakness — running in it himself, against a field of horses. He took Doris's seat, frowning disapprovingly at the overflowing ashtray.

"How's it goin', Steuben?" he asked breezily.

Taking a moment to adjust, all I could think of was Doris and the Coneys she had promised to get me.

"Just waiting for Doris to return," I replied finally, uncomfortably.

"Ah yes, Doris. She is most obliging," he said in a somber tone. "Was she, ah, disturbing you?"

"Disturbing me, what do you mean?"

"It's apparent that she spent quite some time here by your bedside."

"She was on her break," I quickly said in her defense.

"Oh, was that it?"

"Yes it was, but why are *you* here, Doctor?"

"Me? Why am I here? Heavens, Steuben!" he replied indignantly. "I work here. I'm the head psychiatrist in the Institute."

"You're the 'head shrink'?"

"Well, if you want to put it that way."

"Okay, Doctor, then tell me, why are you, a psychiatrist, and Dr. Weidelman, for that matter, so interested in me, in so much as I have a physical injury to my head? Why am I not in a regular hospital under the care of a normal doctor?"

"Ah yes, Steuben, but you have been *committed* here. Has Dr. Weidelman not informed you of that fact?"

"No! Not in so many words," I replied firmly, "and who committed me here? I've been told that I have no known relatives and almost no real visitors, only my agent. Good God, it wasn't him?"

"Oh no, in fact, Steuben, it was me, on consultation of course with the rest of the medical faculty."

"You can do that?"

"Yes, Steuben, we can. And we had solid grounds to do so. The fact is that you haven't been totally comatose over the last few weeks. There have been short periods of what one could refer to as 'alertness.'"

"Alertness?"

"Yes, and in those periods of alertness you spoke of, well, you spoke of an invasion of the planet by little blue men. Need I say more?"

"It wasn't exactly an invasion," I replied in my defense.

"There you go again. You also babbled something about Mongolians threatening the planet."

"Oh, they weren't Mongolians from Mongolia; they were Mungoliens," I replied, emphasizing the "u."

"Well, now, that does make a difference, doesn't it?" replied Dr. Zloty, sarcastically. "And who is this 'Pymm' character. His name kept cropping up during your periods of babbling."

"Oh it's 'babbling' now, is it? As for Pymm, he's the little blue man who first visited me."

"And where did this visit occur?"

"I first met him when he rapped on my apartment door."

"And where was this?"

"Linksville, B.C."

"Linksville, eh? I'm sorry to inform you, Steuben, but we checked it out. There's no 'Linksville' in B.C. or anywhere else in Canada."

"No?" I cried. "My God, it's the Chain-link Capitol of the Universe, according to Mulligan."

"Who's Mulligan?"

"Oh never mind!" I snapped irritably. "No offense, Doc, but I don't trust you. Who else was present during my 'babbling'?"

"Doris, mainly," replied Dr. Zloty.

"Not Dr. Weidelman?"

"No. Actually, I was more interested in you than Dr. Weidelman was, at least, in your babbling. So, you say that these Mungoliens have infested the planet?"

"Good God no!" I shrieked. "I never believed a word of it. That was just what Pymm said. And it might interest you to know, that we agreed to call them 'Mungo Beings' and not 'Mungoliens.'"

"It doesn't, so I won't ask you 'why?'"

"Frankly, Doc, I think Pymm was a bit paranoid."

"And where did you say Pymm was from?"

"I didn't say, unless I babbled it. He's from the planet Paranoia."

"Ah yes, of course. It all makes sense now."

"It does?"

"No, Steuben, it doesn't," replied Dr. Zloty, grimacing, "but we're trying, aren't we? Tell me more about this Pymm character. During one of your 'fantasies' you mentioned something about a trip to Nevada."

"Ah, so now it's 'fantasies', is it? And yes, Doc, that was quite an adventure."

"You referred to something that you called '*Crossings*'?"

"Yes, well, there were two separate spaceships, the *First Crossing* — which was wiped out, by the way, at least the two Paranoians on board were — and the *Second Crossing* bearing both Pymm and his *sensuum* mate Poothy."

"Poothy? Was he another one of those little blue men?"

"Oh no, Poothy was — *is,* actually — a little blue woman, definitely a woman. I didn't mention her during my babbling, did I?"

"Not that I can recall."

"Was I reasonably coherent during my, uh …?"

"That, Steuben, is what truly fascinates me," replied Dr. Zloty, more animatedly. "Yes, you babbled, but in fragments, separated by relapses into a coma — but the fragments were remarkably connected, coherent, and detailed. I have to admit that though what you babbled about was patently absurd, you sounded rather convincing."

"Doc!" I cried, sparked by Dr. Zloty's renewed enthusiasm. "Would you allow me to pinch you just to make sure that you are real?"

"Is that necessary?" replied Dr. Zloty, with a frown. "It seems that your pinching Dr. Weidelman would have been enough?"

"It would help me, Doc. I do feel terribly insecure."

"Well, if it helps," he replied, offering me his arm, diffidently.

His skin was an odd color, slightly bluish in tint — though it might have been the light — and entirely unblemished. I gave it a fierce pinch, rendering it no longer unblemished.

"Was that necessary?" he shrieked, jerking his arm back.

"Sorry," I said, "but, to be honest, Doc, what you appear to think of as fantasies seemed more real to me than this hospital room."

"Did the pinch help at all? It's not standard procedure."

"Yes, a bit, but I did far more than pinch during these so-called 'fantasies.' I talked to Pymm, met various people from the town of Linksville, attended a radio talk show, journeyed in a spaceship to Nevada, and well, there was a lot more to it than pinching."

"So you say. Please tell me more, and don't spare the details."

And trustingly, I told Dr. Zloty all that I could recall about my meetings with Pymm, the misadventures in Linksville, and the trip to Nevada — even about the *sensuum* and the "affair" with Poothy — and of course, the spaceship's mysterious source of power — the *orgasm*.

Dr. Zloty listened with the gaping bewilderment of a child given a lecture on metaphysics, until I mentioned the word "*orgasm*", wherein, he seemingly had a psychological *orgasm* of his own — if there was such a thing.

"Come, come, Steuben, surely you see how absurd all that is?"

"Well, Doc, I must say, that the entire 'Netherman episode' was extraordinarily convincing, more so than my experience here."

"If you say so, Steuben," muttered Dr. Zloty skeptically. "Now, tell me more about this old prospector that you encountered."

"You mean Old Mundy?"

"Yes. And I must say at the outset, that it is a bit of a coincidence that you are here now in the Mundy Institute."

"It was a surprise to me, too, Doc," I replied.

"So tell me, you maintain that this old prospector single-handedly massacred all the aliens from the first spaceship, the one you call the *First Crossing*?"

"Yes, I do, but there were only two of them, Elsymm and Broom. They were *suum-mates*."

"I'm going to let this *suum-mates* thing pass," scowled Dr. Zloty, "but what wonderful detail, wonderful detail. And you say that the Paranoians that you actually encountered, Pymm and Poothy, returned to their planet Paranoia on the *First Crossing*?"

"Right, Doc. They left Earth with several earthling specimens."

"Specimens? What kind of specimens?"

"The human kind."

"You mean people?"

"Yes, including some folks from Linksville."

"Wow!" cried Dr. Zloty. "What an impressive tale!"

"It's not a tale. It really happened."

"Sure, sure, Steuben."

"It was real, Doc," I protested. "Come now, a prolonged
experience without gaps, and in vivid detail. It couldn't have
been a dream — could it?"

"Good, good, Steuben, as long as there is doubt. We can
build on that," replied Dr. Zloty, soothingly. "But tell me, this
'orgasm' you refer to fascinates me. How did that work again?"

"Oh that. I don't understand the technology of course. It's
advanced Paranoian stuff, but *les saucers* — Pymm liked calling
them that, with the French pronunciation, of course — were
somehow propelled by *orgasms*."

"Paranoian *orgasms*?"

"Yes, but possibly earth ones as well," I offered — once again
haunted by memories of the *sensuum* on the *Second Crossing*.

"Maybe the word means something else in Paranoian,
something more connected to normal physics?"

"I don't think so, Doc. I experienced it 'first hand.' Crazy as
it sounds, I'm sure I helped propel the spaceship to Nevada."

"Right, right, sure, of course! What else could it have been?"
replied Dr. Zloty gleefully.

"Can I ask you a personal question?" I asked. Then, aware of his uneasiness. "Oh don't worry, Doc, it has nothing to do with orgasms."

"Oh that is a relief," he replied, laughing boisterously, attempting to make a joke of it.

"It's just that your name is strange. It doesn't seem real. Isn't a 'zloty' a Polish monetary unit?"

"Yes it is, in fact, still, it's a rather common surname in Poland."

"And this *Lekarz* on your name tag, doesn't that also mean 'doctor' in Polish?"

"It does, how do you know that?"

"A taxi driver told me. He was a *lekarz* back in Poland."

"There are a lot of *lekarze* back in Poland."

"I'll take your word for it, Doc. So then, in a sense you are Doctor Doctor Zloty?" I continued.

"You know, Steuben," sighed Dr. Zloty, "you're the very first person to notice that. It's a somewhat embarrassing story, but when I first arrived at the Institute, I told the duty nurse that I was 'Lekarz Zloty,' so she made up my name tag as 'Doctor Lekarz Zloty.'"

"And you didn't correct her?"

"No. You don't argue with duty nurses. But look here, Steuben, this isn't about me, it's about you."

"Okay, Doc, if you say so."

"And please, don't call me 'Doc,' I find it irritating. Now where were we?"

"I think you were about to leave," I replied suggestively.

"But we've barely begun," insisted Dr. Zloty. "What I don't get is this belief you have that all these experiences you refer to are real. Yes, the brain is a marvelous and essentially unexplored territory offering up surprises every day, but in your case, I mean, well, it's extraordinary."

"You should write a paper about it, Doc, I mean, Dr. Zloty."

"Yes, I've been thinking about it."

"Do you normally get involved with specific cases?"

"No, Steuben, I'm more of an administrator these days."

"You sound bitter."

"Well, administration certainly isn't that interesting. I much prefer poking into people's heads, so to speak."

"Why not delegate more of your routine duties?" I suggested.

"I suppose I could," sighed Dr. Zloty. "But ah, here we go again, talking about me when you are the patient. Look at it from my point of view, Steuben. There's undeniably a lump on the back of your head."

"Wait a minute, Doc. If the incident, this mugging, occurred about two years ago, why is there still a lump on my head?"

"Ah. That is a good question. I'm not sure why, but the lump comes and goes."

"It comes and goes?"

"Yes."

"Is that a good thing?"

"I don't think so."

"Oh well, please go on with your story."

"Thank you, Steuben," replied Dr. Zloty with a hint of sarcasm. "As I was about to say, scores of witnesses have attested to the mugging in the park and your stay in both St. Agnes' and here in the Institute. And all of this is over a considerable period of time. Then there's your driver's license confirming that you are indeed a Mr. Lester Steuben. All these are pretty much facts, and inconsistent with the stories you tell. How do you respond to that?"

"Why do you think I want to pinch you, Doctor, and the others?" I almost shouted. "I know I'm real, it's *you* I'm worried about."

Dr. Zloty sat back in his chair, hands clasped behind his head for support — as though his head was a massive burden.

"So you think that I might not be real, is that it?"

"I have my suspicions."

"Well then, it seems that we're back at square one, and that might be an appropriate place to end today's session. Do you mind if I stay for a moment and take notes?" he asked, reaching for a black book inside a pocket of his white gown.

"You don't make notes back in your office?"

"Yes, but I feel that being here in your presence might help."

"I don't understand, how?"

"There you go again, Steuben, making it about me again. Oh well, if you must. In my early days as a practicing psychiatrist, I always stayed with my patients for a few moments afterwards, and made notes. Gradually, I broke away from the practice."

"Why, may I ask?"

"It didn't seem professional."

"You could be right about that."

"In any case, Steuben, you're a special case. Humor me."

"So you're going to look at me and make notes?"

"Right, if you don't mind."

"Knock yourself out, Doc."

"Thanks, Steuben."

With a stubby pencil, Dr. Zloty began making notes in neat block letters, childlike in his determination, peering at me occasionally, lost in deep learned psychological analysis — until he finally fell asleep.

And, soon afterward, so did I.

Chapter 22 – Poothy

I MUST HAVE LAPSED INTO another one of those cursed comas, or blackouts, or whatever they were, for I awoke with a headache, seated at a round table in the middle of a lush oasis surrounded by desert, my head resting on its surface in repose.

Was I back in Nevada? I wondered, but only for an instant.

The sand was different, finer, softer, and there were small clusters of trees, tall and stately, with enormously broad flapping leaves. I reached over and touched the bark of the nearest tree; it was thick and rubbery. The nearby bushes drooped, seemingly weeping. The sky was deep sea green and lightly misted over, not like on Earth, but patterned — as though painted by an artist. The sun shone brightly, but not burning, kinder than an earthly sun.

A hand touched my left shoulder.

I jerked upright.

Poothy appeared from behind me carrying a broad orange parasol. She sat opposite me, laying the parasol down upon the table.

"Hello, Noothy," she said softly. "How are you feeling?"

"A bit rested, but my head hurts and I'm very confused," I replied. "Where are we? It seems to be Paranoia, but…"

"Of course it's Paranoia, Noothy. We moved you here to the Stone Oasis for more progressive treatment. Don't you remember? It has only a few patients, all with severe mental disorders. Tragically, the population of Paranoia is on the verge of extinction and everyone's survival is critical."

"Please, Poothy, call me Netherman. I'll even accept Steuben but not Noothy," I pleaded. "And I'm truly sorry about your planet's plight, but I'm an earthling, and I have no idea what I'm doing here — if indeed I am even here."

"Pshaw! You're Noothy," she hissed, "and you'll just have to accept it. It's vital to your recovery."

Evidently, there was no arguing with that, so, reluctantly, I silently acquiesced.

"And if you're wondering about Pymm," she continued, "he's off visiting a spa on a neighboring oasis. The last few days have been rather stressful for him — and you're mainly to blame. It's soo sad. He hasn't been himself lately."

Stressful for him? I'm to blame? I thought. *What about me?*

At that moment a shadow swept across our table. High above us a huge bird made a long, curving arc.

I shivered instinctively.

"Oh don't be afraid," murmured Poothy. "It's only a *burgee*."

"But that's the thing that sat on me," I protested.

"That's only Pymm's theory. I don't believe it happened. *Burgees* are timid creatures."

"It doesn't look timid," I said questioningly, but the *burgee* had fled away and I relaxed. "I thought that there was very little sand on Paranoia," I said eventually, peering out beyond the oasis towards a vast stretch of desert.

"Where did you get *that* quaint idea?" murmured Poothy.

"Pymm said so, back on Earth."

"Back on Earth! Oh, Noothy, you're regressing," moaned Poothy. "Look around you. Paranoia is nothing but sand, with a scattering of small oases."

"With weird trees and bushes," I offered, with a nervous laugh. "And where are these other people Pymm said I was supposed to meet? So far, you and he are the only ones I've spoken to. It truly makes me wonder — if *this* is all a fantasy."

"Pymm and I had a long discussion about your case, Noothy," she murmured, her slender fingers sensuously riffling through the folds of the parasol. "And speaking of 'fantasies,' he told me about your two highly imaginative identities back on that fictitious planet you call 'Earth.' Who were they, Noothy — Netherman and Steuben? What ghastly names!" She leaned towards me with a sudden urgency. "My dearest, Noothy. You and I shared so much. Don't you remember any of it?"

"You mean the *sensuum* on the *Second Crossing*?"

"Oh, Noothy," she sighed, with evident disappointment. "There was no *First Crossing* or *Second Crossing*. We don't even have spaceships on Paranoia."

"There are no *saucers* on Paranoia?" I cried.

It was, well, incroyable!

"None, and why would there be? There are so few of us that the idea of leaving our planet, abandoning it if you will, is, well, unthinkable. And this idea of an *orgasm* propelling these *saucers*, well, how mad is that? I must inform you, as your doctor and friend, that there is no such thing as an *orgasm* — of any kind. This fixation of yours has to stop! It's all so sordid and simply makes me shudder."

"There are no *orgasms* on Paranoia?" I gasped.

"None."

No saucers and no orgasms!

I was devastated

"But you do have *sensuums*, don't you?" I asked pleadingly.

"Yith, we do, but they're not the barbaric contrivances that you described in your fantasies. For one thing, there is no physical contact between *suum-mates*, just a spiritual consanguinity of sorts."

"I have no idea what that means," I replied.

"In time, you'll get better, you'll understand."

"But it was all so vivid," I protested, not for the first time.

"Check your so-called 'nether regions,' Noothy. See what you find, if anything?"

"I don't have to check, Poothy," I replied, laughing riotously. "I'm quite aware of my own body, thank you."

"Oh, Noothy!" she murmured despondently. "How can you not remember when you and I were *suum-mates*, true *suum-mates*?"

I turned away, unable to withstand her fiery gaze. Of course, she was talking nonsense, but there was no doubt of her deep conviction.

"Sorry, Poothy. I-I don't remember," I finally replied.

"We *were* once *suum-mates*, Noothy, and then that scoundrel Pymm stole you away — and you and he became *suum-mates*."

"Me and Pymm?"

"Yith. And now each of us wants you back. Soo, Noothy, you will eventually have to choose between us — when you have recovered from your traumatic condition, of course."

"You mean from the attack in Central Park?"

"Good *Goor*, Noothy. I thought we were making progress! Well then, let's take this one step at a time, shall we?" she replied, taking on a more serious demeanor. "Do you now have a lump on your head?"

"No," I said, once again checking the top of my head.

"And during your 'Institute fantasy,' there was a lump?"

"Yes," I admitted, "a rather sizable one."

"Soo, it's not there now. What does that tell you?"

I hesitated.

"It comes and goes?"

"You'll have to try better than that."

"Okay, how about that I was either dreaming then, about the lump, I mean, or dreaming now?" I replied.

"And what is your deepest belief?"

"You'll find it strange?"

"Oh for *Goor*'s sake! We're far beyond strange!"

"Well then," I replied, gathering my thoughts. "What I think is that Pymm returned to Earth and kidnapped me."

"When did he do this?"

"After leaving Earth in the *First Crossing* — with you and his earthling specimens — he returned and ..."

"Captured you against your will?"

"Yes, using this *quarrking* thing."

"What in all the galaxies do you mean by this 'quarrking thing'? Oh never mind! But why would he do such a thing?"

"You said it, Poothy. Paranoia is on the verge of extinction. The two crossings ventured to Earth to collect earthling specimens."

"Specimens?"

"Yes, Rufus Mulligan and me, among others."

"Good *Goor*, what for?"

"Why to turn us into Paranoians, obviously," I replied. "It's a slow process, I'm sure, but look at my skin. It already has a bluish tint. You want to repopulate Paranoia with transformed earthlings!"

Poothy stared at me, then shrieked, at least I thought it was a shriek, but soon realized that she was laughing, that chilling skin-crawling Paranoian laugh of hers.

"Oh, Noothy," she finally replied. "You have such a wonderfully inventive imagination. Maybe that's why I-I ..."

"You what?" I snapped.

She was an annoying, irritatingly twisted woman, and still — I could not forget sharing the sensuum *with her.*

"Well, ultimately, Noothy, you will eventually have to choose between us as to who will be your *suum-mate*. Pymm has issued an official lien on you, which means — that you can't be with anyone until the matter is settled."

"But Pymm's a man," I objected.

"Oh, Noothy," she moaned, "that's part of your illness. There is no physical man-woman distinction on Paranoia, no 'nether regions.' Men and women are determined by the way we think and feel. Just examine yourself for *Goor*'s sake!"

What's happening to me? I anguished — refusing to endure the indignity of lowering my head to examine my "nether region."

Of course, I was a man, a normal man. Was she mad?

What about the sensuum *on the* Second Crossing — *and my countless experiences long before that, not to mention Doris and the Institute?*

Sukh wasn't the only one "to go thump in the night."

"It's both sad and wonderful, Noothy," continued Poothy, "how our Paranoian brains are so powerful with a remarkable facility for detailed and realistic fantasy. But normally, we don't get trapped into our own fantasies. Somehow, and it does happen to the most gifted of us, you got trapped."

"I got trapped?"

"Yith. Into some primitive fantasy, primitive possibly because of some hidden stress in your life — Pymm thinks it's because a *burgee* sat on you, but that's clearly absurd — and so, out of desperation, out of survival essentially, you had a need to escape, and so you constructed this crude 'Earth fantasy' of yours, with such amazing detail."

"What kind of stress do you think I was under before…?"

"I don't know for sure, but my hypothesis is that you were concerned by Pymm's advances towards you — challenging our uniquely sublime and transcendental relationship."

"When we were *suum-mates*?"

"Oh, Noothy, you do remember?"

"No, I don't. I'm just repeating what you told me earlier."

"Oh! How disappointing," she sighed. "Then there was the stress of facing Paranoia's extinction. You are more sensate than most and so more vulnerable to a breakdown. At least that is my theory."

"But, Poothy, are you aware that, at this very moment, we are communicating using earth-speak?"

"Are we speaking, Noothy, are we really speaking?" she murmured, chilling me to the bone.

Chapter 23 – The Institute, or Is It?

I WAS LYING ON MY back, dreamily conscious, eyes closed — with the scent of lavender in the air.

Where was I? And how had I got there? I wondered.

My last memory was of Poothy, not only questioning my manhood, but even whether we were speaking or not.

But where did I want to be? I anguished.

Earth for sure, anywhere but Paranoia.

But who did I want to be, Netherman or Steuben? It had to be one or the other, did it not? Or was it possible that I could be someone else, some other earthling?

Oh God! That was a path I dared not tread.

With eyes kept purposely shut, I struggled with the question.

My earliest memories, which admittedly did not go back very far, were of Linksville and Netherman, but the Steuben identity was far more detailed, far more convincing. It included a Greek landlord, a literary agent and even a driver's license — with a birth date and a home address on it — as well as records, presumably, of my two-year stay in the Institute. As I digested what I knew, I quickly realized that I was now strongly leaning towards being Steuben.

I had never really liked Netherman anyway.

Screw his Bulgarian teacups.

I finally opened my eyes and my entire body relaxed. I was back in the Institute and Doris was by my side. I tried to rise but couldn't.

"Don't struggle, hun," she said.

"Why can't I get up?" I cried.

"You're strapped to the bed, love," she said unctuously, "to prevent you from injuring yourself."

"Untie me, untie me!" I shrieked.

"Right, hun, just relax. I'm unbuckling the straps now."

"What happened?" I asked when the straps had been removed. "Why was I strapped to the bed?"

"You had a terrible nightmare last night, a most horrible nightmare. Don't you remember any of it?"

"No."

"Well I've told Dr. Zloty that you've regained consciousness. He'll be here shortly. He's eager to resume your sessions."

"Sessions?"

"Yes, love. Surely you remember your recent sessions with Dr. Zloty? He was so pleased with them."

"No, I don't," I bellowed, "all I remember is one or two meetings with Dr. Weidelman, and one with Dr. Zloty — he was taking notes in his black book with that stubby pencil, last I remember."

"And you don't remember our, our — little trysts?"

"Trysts?"

"Between us, love, there were several of them. But I'm not sure we should be talking about *them*. They were somewhat — intimate."

"You have to tell me about them, Doris. Good God! I've got to know what happened."

"Well then, if I must," she said sitting on the edge of the bed, disturbingly close. "The first time was when we had a conversation about, well, it was about sexuality. You were wondering whether you were normal."

"Normal, in what sense?"

"You were wondering whether you had homosexual tendencies."

"Tendencies? And did I?"

"No, love. Don't be upset," she replied, with a matronly pat on my thigh. "I convinced you that you didn't."

"And how did you do that?" I groaned.

"Well, hun, since you ask," she said, almost shyly, "I seem to have a talent for testing men."

"And you applied this test to me?" I asked, with alarm.

"Yes, love."

"And what is this test, Doris?" I asked, dreading her response.

"No need to be upset, love," she replied, a flutter in her voice. "I would never take advantage of a patient, though you're not just any patient. You know that, don't you, hun?"

"It's been a suspicion of mine," I replied, trying to remain calm. "Now, Doris, tell me, what exactly is this test?"

"Oh it's simple, really. I merely stroke your arm, slowly, softly, elbow to wrist, occasionally tweaking a hair. That's all."

"And you can tell from that?"

"Yes, love."

"How does it work?"

"Well, when I stroke a man's arm — a real man's arm — there's usually a reaction."

"What kind of a reaction?"

She sighed.

"They get hard, hun, they get hard," she said finally.

"Oh God, you mean they have an erection?"

"Yes, love."

"And did I?"

"Yes, love."

"Oh my, so I do have a nether region?"

"That's an odd way to put it, but of course you do, hun."

I was unable to look at her directly. Not only was her mere presence, intimidating, but the personal scent of lavender was intoxicating. Surreptitiously, I slipped my hand under the sheet testing my "nether region" and was pleasantly relieved.

"Don't be upset, love," she continued, "after all, I am your nurse. And in my personal experience, more often than not, a special bond develops between an unconscious male patient and his nurse. After all, we have to tend to your bedpan, and, and…"

"Yes. I understand, Doris, and oh... I just remembered. What about the two Coneys you promised me?"

"Oh, hun! You ate them! You don't remember?"

"No," I muttered, dejected. "I'm surprised. It's something I thought that I would remember."

"Well, love, you certainly did enjoy them, and oh yes, I put the sign on the door that you requested."

"What sign?"

"The sign that says 'Straight Men Only.'"

"I requested that?"

"Yes, hun, after our last tryst."

And that, mercifully, was when Dr. Zloty walked into the room.

Doris hustled out seemingly glad to do so.

The mood immediately changed. My skin began to crawl — and not in a good way.

"Ah good to see you so alert, Steuben," he said breezily. "Have you been exercising as we discussed during our last session?"

"Sorry, Doc, but I don't remember our last session, only the one that ended with you making notes in your black book."

"Oh dear," replied Dr. Zloty slipping into the bedside chair. "A minor setback then, but there's good news on the physical front."

"You mean my arms, legs, and all of my other appendages are functioning properly?"

"Strangely put, but yes, and during our recent sessions *we* have even managed a short walk, or two, in the nearby park."

"You and I, Doc?"

"It's Dr. Zloty, Steuben, and no, not you and me. As you might suspect I'm a rather busy man. Doris accompanied you on your walks. But, apart from last night's setback, you have appeared encouragingly normal of late, sleeping peacefully, coherent while awake — with none of those annoying references to strange aliens, or that sort of thing."

"You said you're busy, Doc, but it occurs to me that this place is rather quiet. In fact, apart from Doris and you, there doesn't appear to be anyone else in the building, no other doctors, or nurses — and I haven't even met Oya yet."

"Who's Oya?"

"The Bornean attendant who bathes me, according to Doris."

"Hmm. I've never met her."

"I suppose she only bathes patients and not doctors."

"Still, I'm curious."

"About what?"

"How a Bornean managed to get into the Institute."

"Oh. And I still haven't seen another patient."

"It's a small ward, Steuben."

"And where are Doctors Weidelman and Shim?"

"Oh them!" replied Dr. Zloty dismissively. "They've gone. We never really needed them anyway. Dr. Weidelman transferred upstate and Dr. Shim returned to Philadelphia. He wasn't really a doctor, you know."

"What was he?"

"We really don't know."

"So you are my only real doctor now?"

"Yes, it's simpler that way. But aren't you curious about what I've discovered? Not only have we been having wonderfully productive sessions, but I have also been busy continuing my investigation of your past as well."

"Sure, Doc, fire away," I replied apprehensively.

"Well then, Steuben, you might be pleased to learn that I have uncovered the hospital in which you were born, and your actual birth certificate. Would you like to see it?"

With trepidation I reached for the small white piece of paper Dr. Zloty thrust towards me. Facts were what I needed, concrete facts.

It wasn't a birth certificate, exactly, but a baptism certificate for one Lester Steuben. Apparently I had been born a Catholic in the Sacred Heart Parish of East Boston. Date of birth, September 26, 1939, child of Joseph von Steuben and Mary Withers. Baptismal date, October 19, 1939. The certificate itself, dated November 11, 1945, a few years later, was based on the Baptismal Register of the Church of Saint Brennan.

The document, a simple piece of paper, as it was, had a nevertheless comforting effect. For the first time I fully realized that in all of my "blackout fantasies," nothing had been so specific, so convincing as that document, not even the earlier driver's license.

Netherman's existence — now under deeper suspicion than ever — seemed just an interlude. It had only spanned a little over a week or so, and I had no consistent memory of anything prior to Pymm's knocking on my apartment door. And Linksville itself, and its surroundings, seemed murky. Even the trip to Nevada, now, was somewhat of a dream, though it had felt so real at the time. And my disjointed "visits" to the planet Paranoia were even more suspect.

No, the only convincing item of evidence as to who I really was, came in the form of that simple white piece of paper, and Dr. Zloty — who I had truthfully never liked, and never trusted — was the source of it. It was so promising, and from what Dr. Zloty had revealed, there was more!

"Okay, Doc," I said finally, "you are beginning to make some sense."

"Me, make sense?" replied Dr. Zloty, looking up at me defensively — having been writing assiduously in one of his little black books during my lengthy reflection — with his stubby yellow golfer's pencil.

What generation of book was it now, fourth, fifth? I wondered.

Then I noticed the Roman numeral VII etched on the cover in gold leaf: *A History of Lester von Steuben,* in seven stubby black books — I imagined — taking its place beside Gibbon's *Rise and Fall of the Roman Empire* and *A Short History of the World* by H.G. Wells.

"Please, Doc, tell me more," I said with genuine concern.

"Delighted to do so, Steuben," he replied. "You must be aware that I had limited resources, of course, but I did manage to discover that both your parents had been killed in an automobile crash in 1945. It was during a celebration of the ending of the Second World War. A drunk driver…"

"Oh damn!" I muttered involuntarily.

"Sorry about that, Steuben," replied Dr. Zloty, momentarily recognizing his insensitivity, before launching forward once again. "You were then put into an orphanage, somewhere."

"You didn't find out where?"

"Unfortunately, no. But I soon discovered that a Lester Steuben had been enrolled in Muriel Pritchard's School for the Deaf and Hard of Hearing in South End, Boston."

"Obviously some sort of mistake?"

"Fortunately, yes. Apparently your enrollment was made in error, and after six months, you were unenrolled. I wasn't able to find an explanation for both events."

"How old was I at the time?"

"Well, all this happened in early 1947."

"So I would have been about eight years old?"

"Give or take a year."

"What did you discover next?"

Dr. Zloty lowered his eyes.

"Unfortunately, that's when the trail went dry."

"That's all there is?" I cried.

"I do have the Institute to run," he snorted.

"But surely I must have attended one of the Boston area orphanages, or high schools?"

"I did check two Boston orphanages and three high schools."

"And that's all?"

"It's not easy getting to Boston. But clearly, you ended up in New York. Your driver's license attests to that!"

"What about my agent, the one who visited me?"

"He refuses to talk to me, wants nothing to do with you."

"Shit!"

"And the only other connection with you is that Greek landlord, and again, it is best we leave him out of it."

The account seemed to tire Dr. Zloty. He rose suddenly, yawned, and with a weak, "See yah soon," he left the room.

I was glad to see him go.

For one thing, the way he stared at me gave me the "willies" — and I wondered whether that was one of the reasons I had Doris place the "Straight Men Only" sign on the door.

And there I was alone, finally, with an opportunity to collect my thoughts about what I knew as more or less fact, and what I believed.

Simply put, I was either an earthling named "Lester," be it "Netherman" or "Steuben," or a Paranoian named "Noothy" — the thought of which brought tears of amusement to my eyes.

However, the most disturbing aspect of the Netherman possibility was that I had little or no memories of anything before living in Linksville — though I did believe that I had sent articles to local magazines on speculation and had published the novel, The Earth Eaters.

There just wasn't much else.

As for the subsequent episodes on the planet Paranoia, they were just too ridiculous, too implausible to be true. And during one of those visits, I had even believed — only briefly, as it was — that Pymm had Shanghaied me and had taken me to Paranoia, principally to be transformed from an earthling into a Paranoian — in order to repopulate a planet facing extinction.

How absurd was that?

I broke out into a fit of laughter.

I could hear the sounds of birds chirping in the park outside — earth birds, not those weird *burgee* birds on Paranoia.

And suddenly, I had a deep sense of who I was. Dr. Zloty, with his documents and investigations, had been my savior.

Furthermore, I could sense my pulsating vibrant member with every fiber in my being, irrefutably identifying me as an earthling man!

I was undoubtedly Lester Steuben, a troubled and tormented — even psychologically impaired creature — but an earthling!

Chapter 24 – The Mirror

I OPENED MY EYES AND Poothy walked into the room — the room with the billowing white curtains, the room in the stone hut in the Stone Oasis. Pymm was by her side, looking glum.

"We shall settle this once and for all," murmured Poothy.

"What do you mean?" I cried, rising from the bed.

I was dressed in a white gown and sandals, like the two Paranoians.

"Follow me," she commanded imperiously, and with Pymm in tow, we left the room.

Outside midst the tall, stately trees and the weeping bushes, the sun shone softly. Moments later, we were striding across the white powdery sand away from the oasis.

"Where are we going?" I asked worriedly.

"We're going to a special mountain. Be patient," replied Poothy.

"But why?"

"Why, you ask? Both you and Pymm have been a constant nuisance, that's why. Finally, we are going to resolve your difficulties."

"Does Pymm have problems, too?"

"Yith, Noothy. He thinks he's an earthling."

"Oh my!" I cried — though, for some perverse reason, I felt pleased. "How far away is this mountain. I don't see anything in the distance."

"We won't see anything for a while, then suddenly, it will appear."

And she was right, for two hours later, footsore and thirsty, a mountain did suddenly pop up out of the desert ahead of us.

"Wow!" I shouted. "That was startling. Have you been here before?"

"Noo," replied Poothy. "The mountain is rarely visited. Only a few of us even know of its existence."

"Does it have a name?"

"Not that I know of, but there's a rock on top of it that does."

"A rock has a name — and you think Earth is odd?" I muttered.

The mountain was a flat plateau reminding me of desert mesas back on Earth. After refreshing ourselves from a well at the base of the cliff, we started up a natural stone staircase spiraling up the wall of the plateau. At the top, a white pervading mist blocked the expected view of the surrounding desert.

A short trek led us to our destination — a large black, rock pillar, standing alone and towering high above us — with a perfectly flat front surface that glistened in the mist.

"This is *Goor's Mirror*," murmured Poothy, stopping in front of it, "though some call it *Goor's Stone*."

"It doesn't look like it belongs here," I offered.

"It doesn't. Centuries ago — according to the tales — it arrived from outer space, landing atop this mountain. It took many years to discover that it had special powers."

"Like what?"

"It's a mirror, a mirror of truth."

"What in heavens is that?"

"If one stands before it and stares into its surface, the image one sees will be perfect — and will not only reflect what appears before it, but more. It will reveal the person's essential nature."

"Its *ollagooh*?" I proclaimed excitedly.

"Yith, and even more," murmured Poothy. "There can be no denying what the mirror reveals."

"But it's nothing but a shiny black surface?" I said.

"It requires concentration to open, Noothy. One must first focus one's mind on it for it to open. If all three of us face it and concentrate, it will open more easily, but I will not be standing in front of it, only you and Pymm."

"Why only us?"

"You are the two with problems, Noothy."

"Oh."

"Are you ready to begin?"

"Yes," I replied — more out of curiosity than any hope of divine discovery.

"Noo," murmured Pymm. "I knoow who I am."

"You think you're an earthling, for *Goor*'s sake," hissed Poothy.

"But I yam," replied Pymm, evidently on the verge of another pink fit.

"You must do it. As your doctor, I insist," hissed Poothy.

"Damn!" said Pymm, grimacing, but nodding his head obediently.

"Okay then," continued Poothy, "both of you, approach closer to the mirror and stand as still as you can."

With a short wondering glance at each other, we obeyed.

For some time, we stared at the surface without anything happening. Then as I was about to relax — the mirror began to shine with a new light.

I stiffened with anticipation.

"Keep focusing," hissed Poothy from behind us. "We're very close."

Suddenly, there appeared before us, in the gleaming flat surface of the rock, a clear image of two creatures, each sharply defined, staring intently back at us.

I shivered in shock at the vision.

"What do you see?" hissed Poothy.

"Two human forms," I replied eerily.

"And you, Pymm?"

"As Noothy says, two human creatures."

"Be more specific, for *Goor*'s sake," rasped Poothy.

"A Paranoian — and an earthling," snorted Pymm.

"And, Noothy, who is the earthling?" asked Poothy.

"Can't you see for yourself?" I shouted desperately.

"Noo. I'm too far to the side. Who is the earthling?"

"Oh, thank God, it's me," interjected Pymm. "I am the earthling."

"And, Noothy, what does that make you?"

"Oh shit!" I cried. "I am the Paranoian!"

"Ah, Noothy," murmured Poothy, slowly exhaling — *though I knew that she wasn't actually speaking, none of us were.* "I can see it in your eyes. You've finally come back to me."

The End

Printed in Canada